The MAGIC of ENDINGS

TOM AVERY

ANDERSEN PRESS

First published in 2023 by
Andersen Press Limited
20 Vauxhall Bridge Road, London SW1V 2SA, UK
Vijverlaan 48, 3062 HL Rotterdam, Nederland
www.andersenpress.co.uk

2 4 6 8 10 9 7 5 3 1

British Library Cataloguing in Publication Data available.

ISBN 978 1 83913 210 0

Printed and bound in Great Britain by Clays Ltd, Elcograf S.p.A.

I Would Take You There

I would take you there, to the land beyond the sea,
I would take you there, and all that we would be
Are unremembered echoes, passing through the mind,
Unless they too pass through the arch: those we left behind.

These are the words of that oldest of lullabies. The one that parents sung long ago to children whose dreams were filled with the land of faerie. It goes on to speak of the endless rolling hills, of green, lush forests which never fade, of ice-capped mountains, of villages, towns and cities filled with strange buildings, more grown from trees and earth than built.

In the longest versions of that song, in verses now known to only a few, it speaks of

Those hidden, mystery folk, faces bright with shining eyes,
Whose long lives flit between their world and the land
*   of you and I.*

If you were to hear that song sung on a midsummer's eve, you might just believe that some land out there does exist, a place of wonders, of magic, of faeries.

And you would be correct.

Summer Moon Rises

Jojo Locke lay in the bed that had once been his father's, not sleeping. He had turned out the light some time ago and his brother Ricco was snoring soundly from his camp bed on the floor.

It wasn't the snoring that kept him awake. Or the gentle farts coming from Trevor, his grandad's dog, curled up at the end of his bed. It wasn't the sound of *Mickey Mack's Family Game Show* buzzing from the television in the front room. Or Grandad's throaty coughing. Or Grandma occasionally shouting answers at the TV that couldn't possibly be right (Question to Harold from the Livingstone family: *We asked your brother Clyde to describe you in three words. What did he say?* Grandma's answer: *Kitty cat.*) Or his mum's soft replies to her mother-in-law: 'Could be, Marnie. Let's see what he says.'

None of these things kept Jojo awake. What kept him from sleep was the thought of Dad. His vanished dad.

In other years, he'd spent months looking forward to this trip: finishing school, coming down by train from the London flat where they lived with Mum, to this other world between the shining sea and rolling hills. Grandad picking them up and bundling their things into the back of his old, green Jeep, then joggling down the roads to the cottage in the lane.

But things had changed for Jojo. He had just finished Year 6, he was off to secondary school in September and Jojo had found himself, this year, for the first time really, thinking about the dad he'd never known – or thought he'd never known. Maybe it was all that growing up he'd been doing, knowing that big things were ahead, big changes.

What Jojo knew was that this year, he had not been able to shift his thoughts from the man who'd disappeared when he was five. Instead of looking forward to his summer holiday, Jojo had been dreading this moment: staying in the house that his dad had once called home, where he'd done all his growing up, in the bed he'd once slept in. Right then, Dad was all he could think about. Or perhaps it wasn't Dad himself he thought of but the absence of him.

He was missing. Truly missing. Not just from Jojo's world, but from his mind, from his heart, from all his rememberings.

There was nothing in the huge open space where his dad should be. Nothing but one snippet of memory. And perhaps this more than anything was what kept Jojo up at night: that one memory of a voice above him – a deep voice, an excited voice – and the great big chasms where memories should be.

'Don't worry, little man,' said the voice that Jojo was sure was his dad's. *'Don't look back. It's going to be OK.'*

That was it. The entirety of Jojo's memories of his dad. Twelve words. No pictures, no sign to say who was at the end of that meeting. But somehow Jojo was certain this was his father's voice. The memory had come to him one day when he was leaving school. His friend Bolu had just got into his own dad's taxi. Jojo waved goodbye, tried to turn but found he could not take his eyes from his friend, caught in his father's embrace. Watching them, Jojo felt an ache in his heart, a longing for something unknown or something lost. Then the voice had spoken, clean out of the clear blue sky:

'Don't worry, little man. Don't look back. It's going to be OK.'

It was all Jojo could do not to cry but instead to hurry home. He couldn't ask Mum about it. She didn't talk about Dad. No one talked about Dad.

For about the millionth time since he'd got there, Jojo checked his phone on the bedside table. It was about as useful as a brick here in Dor, the village that time forgot; there was no signal. He wondered if he'd rather have stayed in London. If he'd rather be heading to the shops with his friends than exploring the river with Grandad. He wondered if he'd rather be at Bolu's house, drawing and coming up with their ideas for the perfect comic than running around the park in Dor. Rather be there thinking of nothing much, than here, thinking only of a man he did not know and could never know.

At least then he wouldn't feel this . . . hollowed-out-ness. There was no other word for it. Not just empty but like something was missing, like something had been taken.

He wondered, as he had a thousand times since the voice

had spoken, if the past was best forgotten. There was no good in trying to claw back something that was long gone.

✱

The moon was full that night. And the sky was clear. And if Jojo had gone to the window of the little room he would have had a clear view up and down the lane. He'd have seen the parked Jeep and the old bike resting against the stone wall, the bin wheeled out for the bin man in the morning, the cottage's garden on this side of the road and the big old barn on the other. He'd have seen a lone fox weaving across the field beyond. And if he'd kept watching, he'd have seen his holiday begin to take a strange turn.

It started with a man dressed in black. He seemed to come from the barn across the way to stand in the middle of the road. But no door opened in the barn. He seemed to stare up at Jojo's window, but no eyes could be seen beneath his dark hood; instead a pair of stars twinkled in their place. He seemed then to be waiting, and indeed he was.

In his waiting, the man in black toyed with a little sack attached to his belt. He reached in and pulled out what appeared to be a few specks of golden dust. He put his fingers to his lips and blew and the specks, now free, lifted on the breeze, floated, glowing ever so slightly. They drifted up, spiralled round and found their way to Jojo's window and through a crack between the frame and the sill. In they swam, like dust motes in the sun, dancing the short space across the

5

room and coming to land on Ricco's eyes. Jojo saw none of this.

That night, Ricco dreamed of an endless tea party with a family of talking badgers, a favourite dream of his, which the man in black knew all too well.

His name is the Sandman. He is the keeper of dreams. For a fleeting night, he brings into sleeping sight the longings of human hearts – those desires hidden even to the dreamer. He may, if he wills it, give life to deep-felt fears too. Dreams and dreads which, when morning breaks, are swept away with the coming dawn. Forgotten once more.

The fox, having wriggled through the hedge and out onto the road, arrived at the Sandman, looked up into his starry eyes, nodded once and continued on his way.

'A nice gentleman, that Mr Fox,' said a voice from a small bench beside the man in black, a bench which you could be sure had not been there a moment before.

The Sandman did not answer. He looked down at the curious new arrival.

The person on the bench, for she was a person of sorts, was standing, rather than sitting on the bench, and grinning a wide, mischievous grin. Even while standing she only reached up to the Sandman's elbow. As well as being as small as a young child, the woman was dressed something like a pirate. She wore high, brown leather boots, striped trousers in black and red and what looked like an old, worn, burgundy army jacket, studded with buttons. Over all of this was slung

6

a multitude of bags and parcels. On her head sat a three-pointed hat beneath which her white hair stood out stark against her dark brown skin. Hanging from her ears were enormous, thick gold hoop earrings.

She was, of course, a faerie. Not the pink, glittery picture book kind. She was the swashbuckling, tricksome, real kind.

'You look old, Penperro,' said the Sandman.

The miniature lady grinned and then stuck out her tongue at the man in black. It was a curious expression coming from the small wrinkled face.

'Old indeed, Sandman,' she said, 'so old I can barely remember the last time someone called me by that name.'

The Sandman did not reply. He knew as well as the faerie beside him that there was nothing that she did not remember like it were yesterday. That was her gift. And her curse. He stood silently, watching the cottage.

'I'll be older still before we're done,' said the faerie. 'This will take more than that one spark of memory let loose in sleeping minds.'

At this the Sandman took a long breath. 'Indeed it will.'

'It may take more than we have left to give,' said the faerie. 'More than I have, anyways.'

The Sandman stood silently in thought again. And then said, 'Time grows short and you grow old.'

The very small, very curious lady made an elaborately silly face at the man in black, sticking out her tongue again, raising one eyebrow, wrinkling her tiny nose.

7

The Sandman turned away, returning his eyes to Jojo's window, tutting and muttering something under his breath that sounded distinctly like, *'Faeries.'*

'In there, is he?' said the lady. She'd returned her face to normal and followed the Sandman's starry gaze. 'I see. I see.' As if she saw through the window, through the wall, right through to the boy in the bed. 'He will need a considerable amount of help.'

The Sandman nodded. 'Help him, Penperro,' he said.

'He's ready,' replied the tiny woman. 'It is time.'

If you could have seen the Sandman's hidden face, you would have been sure he frowned at this. 'Our time is nearly up,' he said. 'The light is nearly out. That boy is all that stands between all we are and an end that should never come. It is now or it is never.'

Penperro the faerie turned to him. She had been going to make another face and say that she knew that as well as he. But the Sandman was gone; like the golden dust, he'd drifted up and away.

The little woman stood, looked down at herself and said, 'I'd better get changed first. No need to alarm anyone.' But she did not then reach into one of her many bags. She merely wrinkled her nose and blinked.

Now if Jojo had been watching at his window and seen the flash of light and the transformation that took place, maybe then what followed would have been easier to believe.

Maybe.

Twinkling Eyes

Jojo was not at the window. He lay in bed, worrying about the next day and the ones to come, thinking about the nights ahead in the creaking cottage with Grandad and Grandma, thinking about Mum going back to London, off to work, thinking of hours of the summer ahead. Thinking about Dad, clinging to that one snippet of memory, even though it filled him only with a sense of loss that he'd not felt before – it came over him in waves.

He didn't want it. If that was all he got of his dad, he didn't want it.

'I just wish . . . I just wish,' he whispered there in the dark. 'I could see him. Just once. That I could remember.'

Knock! Knock! Knock!

The sound of the brass door knocker banging against the wooden door was so loud that it was if the cottage itself jumped. 'Widdershins!' shouted Grandma in the front room. Ricco muttered something about crumpets in his sleep. Grandad started coughing uncontrollably. Trevor's next fart came out like a trumpet parp. And Jojo's mum stood bolt upright on the sofa in the living room.

'I'll get it,' she said. Lizzie Locke was a busy woman. She worked every hour she could as a junior accountant at JP Slater's so that every penny she earned could go towards a home and food and clothes for her two precious boys who meant everything to her. They were the world – all she had.

She was a busy woman and a prepared woman. She was always ready. The knocker went and Lizzie leaped upward from the two-person sofa, where she was sitting, sandwiched between her lost husband's parents.

Still in bed, Jojo stayed perfectly still and listened. A strange tingling filled his fingertips. Something was happening – something unplanned, unexpected, unaccountably exciting; a little ball of nervous energy fizzed in Jojo's stomach.

He listened, over his brother's snoring, to his mum muttering to herself: 'Bit late for a delivery,' she said.

Jojo listened as the floorboards in the hall creaked, as the door handle turned and then:

'Hello, Lizzie!' It was a voice he was sure he'd heard before.

'Errr . . .' said his mum. 'Do I . . . ? Who are you?'

'Come on, Lizzie, you remember me.' A little flash of light burst in beneath Jojo's door.

'I remember you,' said his mum in a funny sort of faraway voice.

'I'm Aunt Pen,' said the caller at the door.

Another sort of flash of light.

'You're Aunt Pen,' Mum droned.

'I'm Jojo's godmother.'

A final flash.

'You're Jojo's godmother,' said Mum in that faraway voice.

Something surely was happening – that ball of energy had bounced around Jojo's stomach like a firework and now made its way to his heart, threatening to burst.

Mum carried on in her normal voice. 'Oh, come in, come in. How long has it been? We haven't seen you since . . . since . . . such a long time. Come in.'

Jojo snuck from his bed, crept across the room and pulled the door open a crack. He could only see Mum taking a dark red coat and hanging it beside their own coats. He caught sight of white hair and a black felt hat, exactly like something an aunt would wear. Then he saw the aunt in question. Hanging from her ears were the biggest, thickest, gold hoops Jojo had ever seen.

'Come in, come in,' his mum said again. 'Are you here to stay? It's a bit of a squeeze.'

'Maybe. Maybe. I will see what needs to be,' said the woman, Aunt Pen, as Mum led her down the hall and Jojo got a first full look at her. 'But I won't take up any room. Promise.'

A woman as tall as Mum. Dark, wrinkled skin and white hair like Grandma. She wore a white blouse and a long black and red skirt. Around her neck were dozens and dozens of necklaces, with beads and lockets and pendants on every one which tinkled and rattled and rang as she lightly followed Mum. But the necklaces were not the strangest thing about her. That was her eyes.

Her eyes were as deep and as dark as the night sky but

within them twinkled a light that did not belong in this world – it was as if the stars had come to rest in those eyes.

And as Jojo looked, those eyes turned towards him.

They turned towards him, and Aunt Pen, or whoever she was, grinned and winked.

'I'll not be the least trouble,' she said. 'Promise.' Aunt Pen raised a pair of crossed fingers for Jojo to see.

Trouble.

Beyond the Sea

In the land beyond the sea, the one beyond our world, beyond the beyond, the one which the Sandman and Penperro the faerie called home, nothing looked as it did in that ancient lullaby. Hope and life and light had left the land of the faeries, or to give it its proper name, Elfhaeme.

The cities, towns and villages lay abandoned; weeds sprang up between the cobblestones, walls sagged and collapsed inwards, roofs which had been a living mass of green were now brown and dead. The ice-capped mountains still stood, but above them swirled black and purple clouds, ominous and terrible. The forests had grown dark too; the glades and dry stream beds were choked with evil weeds, which pulled down and devoured the great trees. The rolling hills were no longer green. They were simply grey lumps. The lesser faeries' powers diminished with the waning light and those that hadn't fled to the human world cowered in their dark homes, knowing it would not be long before all the lights went out.

In a western corner of Elfhaeme stood a castle on a rock in an eternally stormy sea – Dinn Ainnhir, the House of the Nine. It was here that all the life, all the colour, all the magic had gathered. That is not to say this place was crowned with life itself. On the contrary. It was hard and grey, like a granite tooth jutting up out of the dark depths in which it stood. But this was the place where all that vivid life and magic had been drawn and used as a sinister power – the power to hold back death.

There was a throne room in that castle. It had nine sides and once had nine thrones, one for each of the nine faerie queens. Three sets of three.

The first and the oldest, Aoede, queen of song. Followed by Melete, the queen of action, mother of the faerie knight, she who is known to many as Caelia Ceridwen. To complete their triplet came Mneme, the one we call Penperro. She is queen of memory.

The next triad are led by Arche Nymphidia, she who commands all beginnings. After her comes Athena Melpomene, queen of strife, known to many as Morrigan Moronoe, bringer of war. The last of the middle sisters is Arato Thelxinoe, also known as Mabivissey. She is queen of endings, bearer of death. We shall hear much more of her tale.

The last three of nine, the younglings, spend much of their time in the human world, tending, growing, surveying all that they create. Titania, queen of the sky. Morgana, queen of the land. And last, the lost queen, Acciona, queen of the sea, known to her sisters as Polperra the young, Polperra the explorer.

Those sisters, three sets of three, have been known to many, in many ages, in many guises. To the Ancient Greeks, they were the Nine Muses of Boeotia. To the many peoples of the South Pacific, they are the great pantheon of goddesses. To the Norsemen, they were known as the Nine Mothers of Heimdallr. To the people of Iceland, they were the nine maidens, daughters of Rán. To the Celts, they were the Priestesses of Annwn, the witches of Ystawingun and the sorceresses of Caer Lloyw. And in Britain they are remembered as the Nine Sisters of Avalon.

Now only two could still be found – one hidden in the house and one banished to the other world. The rest live in memory, waiting to discover their fate. Now there were but two thrones in that great castle. Two empty thrones. Surrounded by great columns and huge, stained-glass windows.

All was quiet within the House of the Nine. All was quiet within the room of thrones. All had been quiet for a long time. Where was the last queen that called this place home? Where did she hide? Nobody could say. No noise betrayed her. But then . . .

. . . a voice broke out, from somewhere deep in the bowels of the rocks.

'JOJO!' the choked voice cried. Then, 'Left him . . . alone.' And finally, 'Must . . . get . . . back!'

There was no answer, no reply, except from the same place deep in the rock, a cracking, a thunderous boom as if something split, something splintered, as if some deep magic was straining, snapping.

Aunt Pen

Jojo did not get much sleep that night at all. At first it was the clinking of cups and the making of tea. Then it was the laughter of Grandma as Aunt Pen told endless jokes. Then, even after all had gone quiet, he lay awake thinking about those eyes, that voice, and the aunt or godmother or whatever she was that Mum didn't remember one minute and did the next.

When he did finally doze, it wasn't to dreams of cakes and tea and woodland animals like his brother had, it was dreams of black chasms. Dreams of falling and falling and never coming out. Dreams of deep places with rocky walls. Dreams of a sleep that never ended. And somewhere hazy and dark and dim, the face of a man that Jojo did not recognise at all and a woman, dark and terrible with flames for hair.

He woke to the sound of his own name being called out of the dark.

'JOJO!'

'Morning,' shouted Ricco, leaping from his inflatable camp bed onto Dad's old bed where Jojo slept. Ricco was wiry and fast, built for running and climbing and jumping. He landed on Jojo.

Was it his brother who'd called his name? It couldn't have been – the voice that had called in the dark was deep. But

Jojo didn't have time to think any longer on this; his little brother was squashing him.

'Urgh,' said Jojo. 'Get off!' But instead of pushing, he grabbed Ricco into a hug. 'What you doing, buddy?'

That's what Jojo always called his brother. Always had. Where had that nickname come from? They didn't know.

The night before was half forgotten now. Jojo knew he didn't feel right. But what that feeling was, he could not say. Not yet.

'Come on. Holidays,' said Ricco. 'Let's go.'

He was off Jojo and bounding across the room in his *Star Wars* pyjamas. *Star Wars*. Jedis. Mind tricks. Something tickled the back of Jojo's brain. Something strange. But what it was, he was still not sure. It stayed just out of reach. So Jojo followed his brother at a slower pace.

Jojo wasn't built for speed. He was bigger than his brother, stronger and broader. Grandad said he should be a boxer like Grandad had been in the Navy. Mum wasn't sure about that though.

Jojo got his build from Grandad and, he guessed, from his dad.

There were no photos, nothing. He was a phantom. A ghost who had passed through their lives. The whisper of a memory.

Mum always said he was lost to them in a faraway voice, but if someone else asked she told them matter-of-factly he had died. There was no body. No grave to be visited.

There was nothing but all the spaces where Dad should have been.

It made sense that Ricco didn't remember – he wasn't even born when Dad disappeared. He had nothing to remember. But Jojo was five when it happened – the nameless something. Five. So where had his memories gone? Six years of memory. Lost? For ever?

Before this year, before that voice had struck him like a bolt from the blue, none of this had struck Jojo as strange. It was as if a dark cloud had hidden his dad, making them all forget.

'Morning, Grandma,' Ricco shouted. Grandma's hearing wasn't the best.

'Morning,' she shouted back. She had Trevor on her lap, staring up at her as if they were deep in conversation. Trevor, in his way, was the kindest of dogs. He'd started the night on Jojo's bed, then snuggled in with Ricco, and finally migrated to the front room where Grandad and Grandma had slept on the sofa; Mum was in their room last night.

Ricco bundled across the room and sat in front of the TV, flicking through the channels to find a cartoon.

Grandad's brimmed hat and brown shoes were gone; he was out for some 'fresh air'. That meant he was walking by the river, up to the faerie mounds and smoking his pipe. Grandma had never let him smoke in the cottage. 'This place smells bad enough with Trevor's bowels the way they are,' she used to say. These days she didn't say much that made sense. Last year, Jojo had been told that Grandma had something called dementia.

The shower was running – Mum, getting ready to head back to London. And there was a soft singing from the kitchen.

There was singing in the kitchen?

Mum in the shower? Grandma on the sofa? Grandad out walking? Ricco right there? Who was singing in the kitchen?

Then it all came back to him. The flashing lights. Mum's strange voice. Big dark eyes. And as if in thinking about them, he summoned them: that pair of eyes, along with the rest of Aunt Pen, leaned in the kitchen doorway.

'Morning, boys,' she said.

'Morning,' called Ricco, raising a hand to wave but not looking up. Was none of this strange to Ricco? So much was still new to a five-year-old; there were always strangers who seemed to know your name.

'You're . . . real?' Jojo said before he could stop himself.

'Don't be rude now, Jojo,' said Grandma. Then to herself, 'You call a boy "Jojo". What do you expect? Not even a real name, is it? Not like Trevor. That's a proper name.'

Aunt Pen stared at Jojo. 'What else would I be if not real, Jojo Locke?' she said.

Jojo just stared back. What else could she be? A flaming Jedi right here in this house. Or a wizard? Or some sort of . . .

'Mind reader?' said Aunt Pen.

19

Jojo's eyes grew nearly as large as the ones he was staring into. That was exactly what he was thinking.

'Who are you?' he blurted.

But as he spoke the click of heels came down the hall followed by a cloud of steam and perfume. Mum was a magician herself.

'This is Aunt Pen, Jojo. She's your . . .'

'Your godmother,' said the woman with the night-pool eyes and the golden hoops. 'Your mother said I should stay and help with you boys for the summer. And the first thing I can help with is breakfast.'

'Breakfast? Wonderful,' said Mum. 'I even have time to spare before my train since Aunt Pen got the boiler working properly.'

'OK, second thing I can help with is breakfast.'

Aunt Pen disappeared back into the kitchen. Mum turned to Ricco, 'Come and have breakfast, Ricco.'

'OK, Mum!' He got up and bounded after her.

Jojo stood and stared. What on earth was going on?

The breakfast that followed was a strange event. There were all manner of things on the table – bacon, eggs, a big bowl of porridge, toast, saltfish hash.

'Just a few things I conjured up,' Aunt Pen said.

Ricco waded in without a care in the world. He was quite happy with a mystery aunt appearing if it meant this sort of breakfast. And Mum seemed to think nothing of it even though Jojo knew full well that none of this food had been in the cupboard yesterday when he and Grandad had made fishfinger sandwiches for dinner.

'Oooh, lovely,' Grandma kept saying, taking plates, sniffing them and putting them back without eating a thing.

Twenty minutes passed at least before Mum stood and said, 'I really must go. Work is calling.'

'Do you have to, Mum?' Jojo said, just as Ricco spluttered through a mouthful of bacon and egg, 'See ya, Mum!'

'I have to go to work, bub. I'll be finished in a week, then I'll be back and we'll have a proper holiday,' Mum said, leaning down and kissing him on the top of his head.

Jojo frowned over at the woman who called herself Aunt Pen. She raised an eyebrow at him. Jojo's frown deepened, his brow knotting into tight little furrows. He looked back to his mum. 'Please, Mum,' he said, 'I just wish you could stay one more day.'

Aunt Pen's raised eyebrow was joined by a grin.

'Oh, darling,' said his mum and bent toward him for another kiss. As she did this, Aunt Pen wrinkled her nose and blinked.

There it was again, that flash of light. Everyone blinked. Ricco said, *'Ooooohhh.'* And at that moment, instead of kissing him, Jojo's mum let out the loudest, longest, wettest burp you've ever heard. It was so powerful, it felt to Jojo like a wind was rushing through his hair.

Nobody spoke. Nobody moved.

Mum stood. Felt her stomach. Her eyes widened. Her mouth opened. And she burped again. Louder and longer.

This time, Ricco laughed. Grandma said, 'Lovely, dear.' Jojo turned back to Aunt Pen.

She grinned at him once more. And as she grinned, wrinkles sprung up on her face – Jojo was sure they hadn't been there before.

Somewhere Quiet

Mum could not stop burping.

Every time she straightened up to say something . . .
BUUURRRPPPPP!

She tried to sit and take a breath . . .
BUUUUUUURRRRRRRRRRPPPPPP!

She lay on the sofa really still and . . .
BUUUUUUUURRRRRRRRRRPPPPPPPPPPP!

In the end she had to call her boss and say she couldn't come in. She'd have to stay home; she was too sick. Except she didn't say that, she said, 'So sor—*burrrppp* . . . ry. I can't . . . *burrrpppp* . . . come . . . *buurrrppp* . . . in. I'm . . . *burrrrppp* . . . sick . . . *burrrpppp!*'

So she just lay on the sofa burping and burping and burping. When Ricco had finished laughing he went back to watching TV.

'Mum, I'll get you a cup of tea,' Jojo said.

'Thanks, dar—*buuuuurrrrppppp!*' Mum tried. 'Darl—*buuuuurrrrrppppppp!*' She tried again. '. . . ling. *Buuuurrrrppppp!*'

Ricco looked up to laugh once more then turned back to his cartoons.

'OK, Mum. I'll just get it, try not to talk.'

Mum nodded. *Uuuurrrrr* erupted from her throat.

Jojo turned to Aunt Pen with a frown. 'I need to talk to you,' he mouthed.

Aunt Pen waggled her eyebrows and stepped into the kitchen.

'You're not my aunt,' said Jojo as he came through the door. Grandma was still in there. She looked up from a large bowl of cornflakes.

'Don't be rude,' she spluttered.

'I need to talk to you!' Jojo said again, through gritted teeth. 'Somewhere quiet.'

'Somewhere quiet?' said Aunt Pen. 'Hmmmm . . . I know just the place.' Jojo did not like the sound of this. He did not like the grin on Aunt Pen's face. And he did not like it when she reached out and grabbed his hand.

He tried to pull away but her grip was iron. She looked into his eyes. 'You want to talk to me, Jojo?' she said. She wriggled her nose and blinked.

This time the flash of light wasn't just in the room, it was everywhere, it was everything. Grandma, the table, the laid-out food all disappeared into that light. It was all Jojo saw, all he felt and for that brief moment, it was all he was. He was just the light and Aunt Pen was the light. They shot through space, they shot through the world and out the other side to a whole new place. They were light.

Then they were not.

It took Jojo a moment to remember who he was and what he was. And even when he'd remembered, all was dark.

'Somewhere quiet,' said a voice. Aunt Pen's, but somehow smaller.

'Wooaaahhhhh . . .' Jojo shivered. 'That was . . . that was . . . What was that?'

'I took you somewhere quiet,' said Aunt Pen.

That was exactly where they were, somewhere quiet. Silent. There was not a peep to be heard.

Before Jojo's eyes was a bleak and empty land. It was grey and dry. The very ground seemed dead. No life. The sky was filled with gathering storm clouds though. Jojo had time to spy a great chasm before him, a chasm which was filled with a dark frothing sea, and beyond that, a rocky island, before a tiny hand took hold of his and all became light again.

All disappeared and was replaced with the glow of life. They shot across the stormy waters. Jojo squeezed his eyes tight shut.

'You can open your eyes now,' a voice said.

Jojo did just that. Very slowly. And found himself standing high up on that rock in the sea that he'd spied. He was teetering on a tall tower of a vast, cold castle. Not the tallest tower: that one stood before him.

'Oh no . . .' Jojo muttered, looking down. His head swam at the great distance beneath him.

Then a hand took his again. 'Come on,' said the voice of Aunt Pen and . . .

They flew once more as light, through a stone wall.

Jojo opened his eyes once more and found himself

crouched with his arms wrapped around his legs, in a room. Of sorts. For one thing it was a very large room, lit by candles. As wide as a school hall – but this room was circular, or close to, maybe it just had many sides – and as lofty as a great church or temple. All around were marble plinths, each with a statue of a boy or man on top. A boy running. A man holding a hammer. A youth throwing a stone. Every statue seemed to have the same face and the same tightly curled hair. Between them were vast stained-glass windows depicting the same figure in other poses. Too many and too varied for Jojo to take in.

There was nothing else in the room, apart from two empty silver chairs to one side and a tiny woman who stood beside Jojo, looking around at the statues. A tiny woman with white hair and dark skin, wearing red and black striped trousers and an old red jacket with golden buttons. The hoop earrings in her ears were big enough to fit her whole head. Around her were slung dozens and dozens of bags and parcels.

'Here we are then. The House of the Nine,' said the tiny woman in a voice Jojo recognised. 'So much loss.'

'Who ... what ... how ... how ... *how*?' spluttered Jojo, then he leaned forwards, hands on knees, wheezing. Wheezing and choking. Fighting for breath.

'How did we get here?' the tiny woman who sounded exactly like Aunt Pen said, looking from the statues to the coughing boy. 'If you can imagine it, we became particles of light for the briefest of moments and travelled as waves almost instantaneously. There're only three ways to arrive here in this world – by light, as we did, though only a few can do that, and that way will soon be shut altogether; through certain doorways between your world and ours, not many of those left though; or by turning thrice widdershins round a faerie mound in the dead of night in the heart of a thunderstorm. Now, you don't want to do that.'

She winked.

Jojo shook his head, his jaw dropping. *Thrice widdershins?* He didn't have time to consider what this meant. He was wheezing, puffing, choking.

The tiny woman just stared at him.

'Asthma,' he panted. 'Need . . . my . . . pump.'

The tiny woman smiled again and nodded. Leaped and flew to his side. Wrinkled her nose. Winked.

Flash. They were light again. Beams. Thoughts shooting, bouncing across field and city, plain and town. He was just one particle of light and he was every particle. He was himself and himself was nobody and everything all at once.

Then again it stopped. And they were back in a room. A room he knew better than any other. A room that now seemed infinitely small. His own room in London: Tottenham Hotspur posters covered the walls, clothes covered the floor.

Jojo's breath was ragged. He reached for his spare pump from on top of the chest of drawers, littered with toys and Lego and books. Put it to his lips and . . . *puff.*

His throat untightened and he took a deep breath as he

27

pulled the curtain open. This actually was his room. There was Crondall Street. There was the concrete football pitch. He could just see the top of his school building peeking above the flats opposite.

He turned to face the woman who'd brought him there. 'That was incredible. Incredible. How did you . . . ?'

'Ah,' said Aunt Pen, the real Aunt Pen, not the tiny woman who had stood beside him in that strange throne room. 'I can do all manner of things, Jojo Locke. *See* all manner of things – here and there and everywhere.' He looked up at the tall woman in her skirt and white blouse. The woman with the many necklaces with all their beads and pendants that he could see now were in the shape of tiny bags and boxes. The woman with the hoop earrings. But he knew she was somehow the same woman as the small creature that had been in that strange hall of statues. He also saw that she looked older somehow, more stooped, not quite as towering as the Aunt Pen he'd met that morning.

'I,' she said rather grandly, 'am a faerie. One of three and one of nine. One of three, the first three – the muses three. And one of the nine – nine sisters, nine sorceresses, nine faerie queens, if you'd believe such a thing. You could call me your faerie godmother if you choose.'

Jojo's mouth dropped open and his eyebrows shot up. 'Wha—' he began. 'I mean . . . like wha–?' But there were no words.

'I know,' said Aunt Pen – a faerie, a queen, his own

28

godmother, apparently. 'I know. A lot to take in. Throwing you in at the deep end. No point mucking about. Thought I'd show you right from the start. Get it into your head, nice and solid. You're not dreaming, Jojo Locke. This is all real.' With that, Aunt Pen picked up a handful of Lego from a box on Jojo's bed and flung it at him. The plastic bricks rained down as real as real. Jojo threw up an arm to protect himself.

'Oi!' he said, still catching his breath.

'All real,' went on the magical woman in the form of an old auntie. 'That great hall that we visited for the briefest of moments was real, and, you will come to find, a dreadfully important place. Dinn Ainnhir, the House of the Nine, the great castle of the queens of Elfhaeme.' Jojo could see that place, it was burned into his memory. The strangest of strange places. 'That took it out of me, delivering us there. I don't think I have the power to go back that way, not until . . . not unless . . . but,' she frowned now, '*you* will go there again before we reach the end. Then, you must go alone.'

'What . . . ?' This was pure mystery to Jojo. What on earth was all this about? But before he had time to say anything, before he had time to think . . .

'Ready?' said Aunt Pen.

She said this while grabbing his hand once more. Blink, and again they were gone.

They were sunlight. They were the morning. They were a beam of breaking light, shooting out to everywhere all at once. This time though, Jojo struggled. As light, he pushed against the light around him. He broke free and all went dark.

When he came to once more Jojo found himself clutching his asthma pump, standing in his pyjamas, amongst the wildflowers and tall grass of the field opposite the cottage.

Beside him stood the old woman. Aunt Pen. Just an old auntie. Except . . . those eyes, those faerie eyes.

Jojo plonked down on his backside, squelching into the mud; his shaking legs would not hold him. 'So that place . . .' he half whispered, half gasped. He wrapped his arms around himself; checking all was real now. 'That wasn't . . . like . . . the real world?'

'Well,' said Aunt Pen, 'that depends on your perspective, does it not? To me, my sisters, to all the free folk of faerie, our world is very much "the real world" as you put it.'

'The . . . the . . . free folk of faerie?' Jojo whispered. It began to dawn on him that he was not just looking at a real-life faerie but discovering through her a whole world beyond his comprehension, a world of legend and myth and magic. 'There's more . . .?' he said.

'Oh, you humans,' Aunt Pen shook her head and tutted. 'Of course there's more. Or there was and . . . will be. We hope.'

Jojo was lost. What did this cryptic statement mean? But he didn't have time to consider. Aunt Pen went on, 'Elfhaeme is a wide world. Many call it home, from the free faerie folk – piskies, spriggans, sylphs and sprites and others of the Seelie

Court, to the gnomic peoples of the underworld – goblins, hoblins, bobbarts, to the giants and the knockers, the mer and the lep, to the solitary creatures who govern all things magic, from the stars to the rolling tides, from the land of dreams to your waking miracles. We might come and stop a while in your world but home is where home is . . . or was.'

Jojo was still puffing, and squeezing his fists together tightly again and again and shaking his head in disbelief or in a desperate effort to sort his thoughts and the pictures that ran through his mind. 'That was . . . that was another place . . . another whole world?'

His own real world of the cottage was just below them: down the slope of the field stood the old, whitewashed stone home.

'Bingo! You've got it! Someone give this boy a medal. Where did you think I was from . . . France?'

Jojo looked up at the old woman. She wriggled her nose and blinked and in the flash of light that followed became the tiny woman, no taller than the little stool that lived in the bathroom back in the flat. Belts and parcels were slung about her. A pirate hat capped her head. Aunt Pen blinked again and she was back to the old woman who'd whirlwinded into Jojo's life the night before. Blinked once more and there was the faerie. A faerie in the flesh.

'What's . . . what's going on?' exclaimed Jojo, gasping, clutching at the muddy ground.

'Nothing much,' said Aunt Pen. 'We're just here. You're

sitting. I'm standing. And that is part of the problem. Time is ticking on. Time is running out.'

Jojo could not fathom what the . . . faerie (he could not even conceive of the reality of that word) was saying. He squeezed his eyes tight shut. 'I am dreaming,' he muttered. 'I must be. It must be. This is all a dream. This is all . . . this isn't real. It can't be. I'm dreaming. I'm dreaming!' He squeezed his eyes shut and muttered over and over again.

Aunt Pen the faerie grinned. 'You're not dreaming, you big bazzook,' she said softly and rapped her knuckles on his head. 'Stop it!'

Somehow she was precisely like an auntie. Even if that is exactly what she wasn't.

He did stop muttering. But he could not stop shivering. 'You're not dreaming. But you are in shock. Here,' she pulled at her bags and parcels, searching for one in particular. When she found it, a small, silver grey sack with a drawstring top, she reached in and produced a tiny gold bottle.

With a flick, she flung it to Jojo.

Between shivers he reached up and caught it.

'Drink,' Aunt Pen said. 'Just a sip. A tiny drop.'

Jojo did not drink. He looked at the bottle and back at the tiny woman.

'Please, Jojo,' she said, her voice falling to a gentle whisper. 'Drink.'

Jojo shivered, shrugged . . . could he believe this? . . . A different world?

He unscrewed the minuscule lid. Steam curled out, but the gold bottle was cold. He sniffed at the contents – sort of spicy and sweet.

He put the bottle to his mouth and sipped. Heat rushed through him from his teeth and tongue and gums, across his face. It flushed down his neck and then ran in streams, gushing, gurgling, till he was warm all over.

'What was that?' he said.

'That, Mr Locke, was Kernowan Moonshine. Brewed in the light of the Kernowan moon. Give it here. A little drop will keep you toasty all day.'

Jojo reached out and handed it back, placing it in the minute hand of the creature in front of him.

He blinked and swallowed hard. 'This ... is ... unbelievable.'

'I know,' said Aunt Pen, looking altogether pleased with herself.

'And you really are ...' He stopped. 'You really are ... a ...' He couldn't say it. He couldn't squeeze the word out, even if he did begin to believe it.

Aunt Pen, the tiny Aunt Pen, stared into his eyes: 'I am a faerie,' she nodded. 'I have not lied to you, Jojo. Apart from the aunt part. My name is Penperro. I am, as I said, your godmother. And we have met before. Long ago, when you were just a little boy, upon the waves not far from here. The memory is somewhere there, in that noggin of yours, along with a thousand others which have been ...' Aunt Pen opened and closed her mouth, gasping like a fish. Like there were words she just could not say. A space where the words should be. Imprisoned words. She got one out '. . . *locked* . . .' before she gave up and went in a different direction. 'You shall see before we are done. You shall see the things I cannot speak of.'

Jojo stared.

Aunt Pen grinned a wide grin. Then without reason that Jojo could tell, she lifted her hand to her ear. 'Hang on, your mum is wondering where her tea is.'

Without another word, Aunt Pen reached out, clutched Jojo's thumb in her tiny hand and blinked.

Taking Flight

Moments later, Jojo was stumbling out of the kitchen, where Grandma still sat, munching cereal, seeming not to have noticed anything.

'That took a long . . . *buuuurrrrppppppp*!' his mum said.

Jojo had in his hands a steaming cup of tea which he sloshed over the sides as he took dazed step after dazed step forward.

'My fault,' said the woman following Jojo. Aunt Pen was back to normal size (or grown to giant size?). 'I was just showing Jojo a thing or two.'

'Not . . . *buuuurrrrppp*! . . . to . . . *buuuurrrppppp*! . . . worry! . . . *buuuurrrrpppppppppppppp*!!!' said Mum.

Then Mum caught sight of Jojo's filthy, mudcaked pyjamas. She frowned. She looked him up and down. She . . . *'Bbbuuuuurrrrrrppp!'*

Jojo ran to his room and pulled on a pair of jeans and his favourite yellow T-shirt before Mum could ask any questions. He slipped his asthma pump in his pocket – who knew what the rest of day would bring? Then he ran back to check on her.

Mum was tough. Mum didn't cry. Mum was a fighter. She'd tell the boys that she had to fight her way through school – no one expected this black girl orphan immigrant to be top of her class. To fight her way through university – her maths department was full of men and boys jostling for position. To fight her way into the world of accountancy after she took a break from work while the boys were young. Now she was fighting to make all their lives work, make enough money to keep everything running, make enough time to keep them all together.

Mum didn't cry. Apart from once a year. Seventh of August. It was a double whammy. The birthday of Mr Jamie Locke, their vanishing dad, and the anniversary of his disappearance. He went missing on his thirtieth birthday.

Not that she talked about it. Not that she said anything about Dad. She seemed to have as little to say as Jojo had to remember.

'Your dad made me fly,' she'd say to Jojo and Ricco. But that was all. That was the sum of the talk about Jamie Locke, the vanished man.

Mum wasn't a big crier, but she looked miserable there on the sofa, unable to do anything without erupting into burps. Her face was dark. Her lips tight. Her eyes red and dim. She drew her eyebrows together. She opened her mouth. A small, sad burp escaped.

'I . . . *buuurrrrpppp* . . . think . . . *burrrupppp* . . . I'll have . . . *buuuurrrrpppp* . . . a bath . . . *buuururrrrrppp.*'

Jojo nodded and said, 'I'll run it for you, Mum.'

As the water cascaded into the metal tub, and Jojo added a few glugs of some green Relaxing Bath Soak he'd discovered in the cupboard, he found himself thinking about the morning, thinking about all that had happened. He remembered what he'd said. *I wish*, he'd said, *I just wish you could stay one more day.* And then . . . well . . . Mum had stayed one more day. This thought, this granted wish, swam through Jojo's brain.

We need to talk again, he mouthed at Aunt Pen when he had returned from the bathroom. She was sitting beside Ricco, who was still watching cartoons on TV.

She made a face in reply. She squinted at him.

What? she mouthed back.

Jojo knew, he *knew*, that she knew what he was saying. Hadn't she read his mind earlier?

Come with me, he tried again.

Me? Aunt Pen mouthed back, pointing to herself and making a surprised face.

'Come 'ere!' Jojo said loudly this time, a little flame of anger flickering in his chest.

'What?' said Ricco. 'I didn't do nothin'?'

'Not you,' said Jojo. 'Watch the cartoon, buddy.'

Ricco turned back to the TV.

YOU! Jojo mouthed finally and definitely at Aunt Pen.

Oh, me, she mouthed in reply and was with him in an instant, flitting across the room, proving herself once again to be far more than just an auntie come to stay.

'You did this,' Jojo muttered. 'You got Mum sick. Didn't you?'

Aunt Pen pursed her lips and thought. 'Hmm. Let's go somewhere a bit quieter.'

'No! No!' choked Jojo, remembering the strange castle, the flight to his room back home, the mud of the field. Remembering and feeling for the first time a little terrified of the faerie godmother.

Aunt Pen let out a short laugh. 'Not like that,' she said. 'Just this way.' She extended a finger and beckoned to Jojo. They walked down the hall to Jojo and Ricco's room.

'Well. It's not quite as simple as that,' Aunt Pen said, sitting on the bed, looking up at a stern Jojo, his hands on his hips.

'I saw it. I made a wish. I said *I just wish you could stay one more day.* Then you did that thing where you blink with your nose all crinkly. Then it happened. Mum couldn't stop burping and had to stay here.'

'OK,' said Aunt Pen. 'That is what happened. Sort of. Thing is, Mr Locke, it's not quite as simple as me just blinking and making things happen. I've got sort of boundaries. Limitations. I don't even really get to decide. There's a bigger plan at work here, you see. I can sort of steer things, if you like.'

Jojo frowned at his faerie godmother. 'What are you talking about? Steer things? Like this is some sort of ship?'

'Well . . . that's not a bad analogy actually, young Locke. A bit of a lost ship. You're all at sea, you see. Have been for many years since . . . you lost your first mate. Need a serious course correction. That's my job. Getting you back on track.'

'Back on track?'

'Getting everything back on track. The Lockes, the Sisters Nine, the whole flimming world. There's more than a little at stake here. Can you not see it? No, I suppose not yet.' She let out a deep sigh. 'It's more important than you could possibly know that we put right something that went dreadfully wrong, that we put the whole grand spinning worlds of reality back on track.'

The boy frowned deeply, part confusion, part anger. The anger won out. 'Back on track?' said Jojo again, his voice strained. He couldn't shout. There was just a wall separating them from the bathroom and Mum, he could hear her burping even as they spoke. But if he could . . . 'Back on track? I don't have any idea what you are talking about. But I do know that you did this. You granted my wish that Mum would stay home.'

'Sort of.'

'So, you can grant wishes.'

'Well . . .'

'Like, if I said, I wish . . .' He thought for just a moment and then the words seemed to tumble out, like he too was not in control but was being forced to follow a path blindly into the unknown: 'I wish I could fly!' Those were the words he could not put back in.

Aunt Pen grinned a wide grin. Her nose began to wrinkle and twitch.

'Oh, me too,' said an excited voice from the door.

Jojo spun on his heel – five-year-old Ricco was standing in

the doorway, his eyes shining – then he turned back to Aunt Pen.

Her grin was if anything wider, she breathed in deep and then . . .

'No, no, no,' said Jojo. 'I was just . . .'

. . . but it was too late. BLINK!

There was flash of light that seemed to fill the room and then, absolutely nothing happened.

Jojo grabbed his little brother. 'You're OK. You're OK.'

'Gerruuff,' said Ricco through the tight squeeze he was being given. 'Course I'm OK. What d'you think?'

'Just . . . just . . .' Jojo started then looked to Aunt Pen, an eyebrow raised.

'Like I say,' said Aunt Pen, 'it's more of an art than a science. Sometimes it's instant and sometimes . . . no, no, this one's instant.' Her eyes had flicked to Jojo's back. And at that moment he felt it.

A sparkle on his shoulder blade, a frisson of electricity, running down his spine.

'Woah!' said Ricco. 'Wooaahh!'

A buzzing tingle strode across Jojo's back. He reached an arm round behind him: where his T-shirt should have been, there was something soft, soft but *spiny*.

'What is going on?' said Ricco.

Jojo spun his little brother round. Feathers, white and speckled with brown, sprang from his pyjamas too, sprouted and grew.

And grew.

'What have you done?' Jojo said. 'What have you done?'

'Me?' said Aunt Pen. 'Me? You need to be more careful about what you wish for. Wishes are not to be flittered away. Think of what it is you really, really want, before you go burbling about flying.'

While she spoke, that buzz, that tingle spread across Jojo's back, across his shoulder and began its descent down his arms, toward his hands. Feathers were springing up all over, and not just that, his arms were getting longer.

He tried shaking them off, shaking and shaking. But instead he found rather than shaking arms, he had flapping wings. He lifted half a metre off the ground and then came crashing down onto a bedside table.

'Woah,' Ricco said. 'WOOAAHH!'

'What do we do? What do we do?' shouted Jojo.

'What is . . . *burrrppppp* . . . going . . . *buuurrrrrppppp* . . . on in there?' shouted a voice from the bathroom. 'Are you . . . *burrrppppp* . . . OK? Jo—*burrrppprrppp* . . . jo? Ricco?'

'We're OK, Mum,' called Jojo, his voice a squeaky rasp, as Ricco shouted, 'Look at me, Jojo!' and with a step and a flap was out of the open window and away.

'I think,' said Aunt Pen, in reply to Jojo's earlier question, 'you'd better fly.'

Memories of the Sand

'RICCO!' shouted Jojo, launching himself forward. He meant to throw a hand out to grab at Ricco, to grasp his fast disappearing foot. But that lunge became another flap and another flap and before he knew it, Jojo too was headed for the open window and the summer sky beyond.

'Look at me, Jojo!' Ricco squealed. 'I'm flying. I'm flying!'

And he was, he really was. He was three metres off the ground and rising, flapping great long wings of white and brown, each sweep of them propelling him forward.

Jojo spun back toward the bungalow, twisting his own wings – if Mum looked out now . . .

No. The bathroom blind was down. But he could hear her: 'Boys? . . . *buuurrrrpppppp* . . . Boys? Are you O— *buuuurrrrrpppp* . . . K? What's going . . . *buuurrrrpppppp?*'

Jojo gulped, still flapping his wings that kept him hovering. He glanced over his shoulder at his disappearing brother. He looked back to his own window where a tiny lady, with grey hair, huge gold earrings and a pirate hat, was grinning out at him.

What could he do?

'We're just . . . we're just popping out, Mum,' he shouted. 'Just gonna get some fresh air.'

'Hang . . . *buuuurrrrpppp* . . . on!' his mum called.

He looked back to Ricco. He was tiny now, a little action figure of a boy, suspended in the sky. He couldn't just hang on. So he didn't.

By some magic, Jojo didn't just *have* wings, he knew how to use them. He turned and flapped and like that, he was away. A big sweeping burst and he had taken to the skies. Up, up and away.

Ricco was some distance ahead, not just flapping but swooping, diving downwards before catching himself and soaring up again, up and up.

'Ricco,' Jojo called, his larger, more powerful wings pushing him toward his brother.

The air was not, as it had always been, simply the space around him. It was now, to his wings, solid. It was a staircase on which he could place his winged arms and propel himself forward. Except when it was water, through which he could swim, he could glide.

He was a bird, a speeding eagle. He was born to fly.

Jojo could not help himself: as his brother turned to see him, he let out a cry of joy and exhilaration: 'Wooohoooo!'

'Yeeahhhh!' shouted Ricco in reply. 'We're flying!'

'We're flying!' shouted Jojo. 'We're flying!' All thought of going after his little brother to bring him back home was gone. Now his heart was set on flying, on plunging through the white-streaked, blue beyond. 'Come on!'

Jojo caught up to his brother and now tagged him and overtook him.

'You're It!' Jojo shouted. Then he flew – beating and gliding, twirling and spinning. Ricco laughed and laughed and flapped after him.

'Come on, bud,' he called after him then waited till his laughing, soaring brother had him.

'Ittttt!' screamed Ricco and tore off and up across the sky.

A flap and swoop and Jojo was after him, joining him in laughing and screaming. And on they went.

If you'd looked up then, from the fields and tracks below, you'd have seen them, high up as two birds, darting and diving, revelling in the summer sun. Something *did* look up, a lot of somethings. A colony of tiny creatures, which, seeing the fun that was being had, rose from a wildflower meadow to join the two boys. Creatures which you would have thought were insects. They were not.

These beings had only got halfway there when the game stopped.

'Look, look,' said Ricco, between laughs and gasps. He was above Jojo. Higher and higher Ricco had gone and he was pointing down now. Jojo, letting the game fall from his arms, and a last chuckle cough out from his throat, followed his brother's finger.

All the world was laid out below them. The cottage and the lane was behind. Hills to the left. The village of Dor, little toy cottages and shops and the train station to the right.

Jojo remembered, somewhere in his head, that he was

afraid of heights. He remembered that fear but he felt none then. The wings made him fearless.

Out in front of them, where Ricco pointed was the sea. Bluer than the sky, a great, flat pond of blue, only broken by the arch of stone which gave Dor its name. It protruded out from the cliffs that bordered the village, hugged the beach at one end, vaulted over the waves. The Door of Dor.

That's where Ricco pointed. The sea. The sun glinted off the gentle ripples.

'Amazing!' Jojo called up to his brother. But Ricco was higher now, higher and higher.

Jojo looked back down to the blue and the beach. The sand swept a long curve beyond the dunes. They never went there. Not to the beach. Jojo realised, as he looked at the great sweeping expanse, that he didn't know why. They went to the town and the hills, to the park, the river and along to the famous faerie mounds. But neither Grandad and Grandma nor Mum would take them to the beach.

The beach. It was a misty fog of lost memory, that place, and now it was as clear a picture as any place could ever be. Jojo could make out small sails out on the crystalline pond. He could pick out individual children with buckets and spades on the sand. He knew he'd been there. But when . . . when . . .

Jojo frowned. His eyes became fixed. Not on anything he saw there now, but on some moment of memory that appeared before him.

His dad. He was sure it was him.

Jojo flapped his wings, hovering, trying to focus on that man dancing in his mind.

Ricco whooped, a long way up now, higher and higher.

What Jojo saw was a man. He saw just his back. A tall, broad man. He blocked out the setting sun as Jojo sat on the sand. The man was a dark shadow against the light. Jojo could see his floppy wet hair, like a mop on his head. He watched him bend and pick up a stone. Then he turned. There was no face he could see. He was just black shadow. But Jojo knew that his father was looking right at him.

'Come on, buddy,' said the memory Dad. 'I'll teach you how.'

Buddy.

That's what he called Ricco. And now he knew why. Now he knew.

A feather spiralled past Jojo's face. But he did not move, apart from his flapping wings. He hovered, letting the memory flitter past him.

He saw it all now. His dad teaching him to skim stones on that very beach. His dad's beach. Maybe that's why they didn't go there.

He remembered skimming his first stone. He remembered his dad picking him up and flying him around the beach.

Another feather passed him, scudding back and forth through the air.

'Buddy,' he heard his father's voice again. 'Buddy, you did it!' His dad made him fly.

Another feather.

Buddy.

Feather.

Feather?

Jojo shook himself out of the memory and looked around at the blue sky. It was not just a few feathers. There were tens of them, maybe a hundred, spiralling and dipping and fluttering down out of the clear.

Buddy! Ricco!

Jojo wasted not a moment longer. 'Ricco!' he shouted and beat his wings as hard as ever. Beat and beat and shot like an arrow upward, searching the sky for his brother. He saw him then, higher than he could have imagined. Another silhouette against another sun. It blazed orange and red behind Ricco as he continued to fly upward. Up and up. Higher and higher.

'Ricco!' Jojo screamed. 'RICCO!' But scream as he did, up his brother went. As feathers continued to rain down.

Surely Ricco could hear him, Jojo thought. The air was clear. There was nothing between the two of them. But higher they went.

It was as if that great red ball burning above called to him, drew him.

'Ricco!' Jojo tried again. 'Come back. You've gone too high!' He felt it now, the heat of the sun on his own wings. He felt feathers come away as if the sun reached down with minuscule hands and plucked them out.

Harder and harder he beat his failing wings, with each

stroke catching up with Ricco. Further and higher they flew towards the sun.

The sun, which seemed now not just to shine down but to stare at them.

'Ricco!' And with that last shout, Ricco's wings burst with a final puff of feathers and from far, far above, what sounded to Jojo like a cry of laughter.

As Jojo continued to shoot upward, Ricco began to drop. Jojo's heart hammered. Sweat coated him beneath his T-shirt. He had moments to think. Moments till the two would meet. Could he just catch him on his back? Catch him and piggyback him down? It was the only plan he had.

Spreading his own ragged wings, Jojo stopped himself and began his own descent. Slowly, not driving downwards, letting himself begin to fall, watching over his shoulder for his plummeting brother. Watching him as you'd watch a football, following its path, ready to catch it on a stretched foot. Only this was no football, which if he missed it, would carry its path onward to the next player or off for a throw-in. This was his brother.

If he could, Jojo would have reached up to wipe the tears which streamed from his eyes. But he could do nothing but strain forward, to keep the limp form of his brother in his eyeline. To try with all his might to make their paths intersect.

Nearly . . . nearly . . .

Jojo spread his wings and tried to glide beneath Ricco. Missed him.

Ricco kept on falling.

'NOOO!' screamed Jojo. 'RIIICCOOOOO!' But there was nothing he could do. Nothing. His own wings were shredded. He did not even think he could stop himself falling: Ricco ahead and he behind.

They fell.

Back down to Earth

The wind battered Jojo as he tumbled downwards, desperately trying to spot his little brother through tear-streaked eyes.

He was sure he could see a dark cloud below. But the sky had remained clear blue as they had played about and flown upward. It could not be a cloud. Or could it? Could it? It was not just dark but speckled with colour – green, brown and grey.

It was not a cloud. Ricco hit it, slowed, then disappeared into a haze.

Now Jojo *did* lift a hand, or a wing, to wipe his eyes. The last of his feathers quickly pushed aside the tears. He opened his eyes as he too entered the cloud which definitely wasn't a cloud.

Tiny hands, thousands of them, grasped hold of Jojo, his clothes, his fingers, his feet. Tiny, tiny hands, attached to tiny arms and tiny bodies.

The creatures which had risen to join them from the wildflowers were not insects. Not at all. They were people, of some kind, far, far smaller than the faerie Aunt Pen. The one holding Jojo's collar, just in front of his eyes, was no bigger than a mouse. A minuscule person, dressed in grass-green, with the wings of a dragonfly.

Jojo did not stop falling, but he slowed as a thousand

hands pulled him upward. Little faces strained. Tiny voices sang out together. He slowed and he slowed and he could see, just below him, his brother slowing too.

'Thank you! Thank you!' Jojo gasped at the tiny woman who strained at his collar and pulled upward. If she heard him, if she understood, she did not show it.

The tiny people and his brother were not all Jojo could see. The ground, the fields and their own cottage still approached quicker than he would have liked. Still they slowed and still the world rose to reach them.

Jojo could see exactly where they were heading. The barn which sat across the road from their grandparents' cottage. They were nearly upon the moss-covered corrugated roof.

Jojo screamed as a thousand tiny hands let go and a thousand tiny people flew away, back to the safety of their meadow. There'd be no falling boys there to rescue.

Jojo screamed as he and Ricco crashed into the ancient roof. The roof cracked and broke. The pair tumbled, finally, onto a burst bale of old, scratchy hay and Jojo found himself staring upward at a blue sky through a hole almost exactly his size.

'Have fun?' said a voice.

Jojo did not turn to look at Aunt Pen. Not right away. He tried to catch his breath. He lay still and breathed in deep. Coughed and choked. He took his asthma pump from his pocket. He took a puff and another, grateful to his past self for not leaving it in his muddy pyjamas.

Finally, he turned to where the faerie, now just in the form of the old lady Aunt Pen, sat on a dry and dusty bale of hay. *'Fun?'* he said, sitting up.

Then he turned to his brother, who was sitting up beside him, shaking his head and grinning. 'That was amazing!!!' Ricco shouted. 'A-MAZE-ING! But how did we . . . ?'

He didn't finish his question as Jojo, knowing his brother was safe, turned back to the faerie. 'Why didn't you stop us? Why didn't you save us?'

'Stop you?' Aunt Pen said. 'Do you think I am in charge? In control? Not I. Save you? Sometime, Jojo Locke, you will have to do the saving. You will have to save your family. And besides, I saw the piskies come for you.'

'Pixies?' Jojo said. 'They were pixies?'

'Piskies,' Aunt Pen replied. *'Piskies.* Not pixies. There are many of them in your world now, trying to see out the falling darkness. Even they, smallest of the Seelie, know that *you* are worth saving. And to your question, young Ricco. How did you fly? Well . . . shall I tell him, Jojo? Or would you like to?'

'Piskies?' Jojo muttered. There was more to see, more to find of this new world opening before him. More creatures like Aunt Pen. More wonders. 'I . . . I . . . can't,' Jojo said.

Ricco was standing now and brushing dust and hay, bits of roof and feathers from his pyjamas. 'Tell me what?'

Jojo stayed sitting. He looked from Ricco to Aunt Pen and then back again. 'She,' he began. 'Aunt Pen . . . she's . . . well . . .'

'Yeah?' said Ricco, his little brow wrinkling.

'Aunt Pen is a faerie.'

And as he said it, the old lady with the white hair sitting on the hay bale, jumped down, and her leap become a whirl of cloth and hair and wrinkled skin and the person that landed was no longer the auntie but the faerie in the pirate coat and hat. The dozens and dozens of bandoliers, sashes, packets, parcels and pendants across her chest jangled as she landed.

Ricco's mouth made a big, elaborate O. 'WHAAATTT!' he said. 'You are . . .'

'A faerie,' the wizened, miniature pirate said.

'AY-MAY-ZING! AMAZING! AMAZING!'

'I know,' replied Aunt Pen, grinning her grin.

Jojo shook his head and sighed.

'Can I make a wish, then? Can I make a wish?' Ricco shouted, leaping and shaking the last of the feathers from him.

'No!' said Jojo as Aunt Pen said, 'Weeellll . . .'

But Jojo carried on the quickest. 'We can't just go making wishes.'

'He's right. Sort of. I do have certain limitations. There is a plan here,' Aunt Pen tried to say but Jojo went on over the top of her.

'She doesn't know what she's doing! She's dangerous.'

'How dare you!' said Aunt Pen. 'I'm not just any faer—'

But before she got further, Jojo said, 'She made Mum sick when all I wished for—'

'Well you weren't very specific, see,' said Aunt Pen. 'And I did make it happen. Mum *has* stayed one more day.'

'OK. OK. How about this. I wish Mum could stop burping.'

Aunt Pen pursed her lips. Thinking. She scratched her head. 'You can't just reverse magic like that. That is precisely the problem we have. Once they're out, things cannot simply be put back in the box, the pieces just won't fit any more. They must be ... completed ... ended ... fulfilled. If I could then I would ...' Aunt Pen opened her mouth in that fishlike way again, struggling with words which were unsayable. 'I would ...' she tried again. Finally, she huffed. 'Some things I cannot speak of. But ... well ...' Aunt Pen fumbled at her necklaces, the little packages and bag pendants. 'Ah ha,' she said and pulled one from the bunch. It looked for all the world like a miniaturised treasure chest.

She took it in her long fingers, seeming to press it here, twist it there. There was a click and a tock and it opened. Aunt Pen reached in with a finger and thumb. She caught something with a, 'Here we go.' She pulled and pulled and out popped a full-size alarm clock, the sort with a bell on top. The sort that could not possibly have fitted inside that tiny pendant.

Ricco's mouth fell open. 'Oh, man!' he said. 'That was amazing!'

Aunt Pen nodded and grinned. 'I know. It rather was, wasn't it.' Then she studied the clock. 'The thing about magic in this world is, it doesn't last all that long. Like your wings. There's a time limit to these things. And those burps that have been inflicted, at your wish, I might add again,' she raised an eyebrow and a finger to Jojo, 'should be stopping right about . . .'

But before she could finish: 'Who's in there?' called a voice they all knew from outside.

Grandad.

'Don't tell him,' Jojo hissed at his brother. Why, he wasn't sure. Apart from, he wondered, he still wondered, if perhaps he was simply going mad. 'Don't tell him.'

'Who's in there? You're trespassin'. I'll call the police.'

Jojo stood and rushed to the door. 'It's us, Grandad. It's us.' He pushed at the rickety, wooden door and there was Grandad, standing in the light of the summer sun.

'What you doin' in there?' he said.

'Jus' playing,' Ricco said, appearing at Jojo's elbow. 'Jus' playing.'

Grandad pushed at the door, letting in more light. Jojo's heart skipped – Aunt Pen – he glanced back but the faerie was nowhere to be seen. 'Well,' said Grandad. 'I guess it is your barn.'

'Our barn?' Jojo said.

'Is that what I said?' Grandad was shaking his head like he was trying to clear a foggy brain. 'Was your dad's . . . I think. He was gonna build . . . a house. Before . . . before . . .' That sentence was not finished. Never finished. 'How did I not remember that,' Grandad growled to himself. He shook his head again and turned back to the cottage. 'Come on,' he said. 'Your mum seems to be all better. Thought we'd get fish and chips for lunch.'

'Woohooo,' said Ricco. 'Best day ever!' and hopped on after him.

Jojo turned, looked back into the barn. There was an old red boat in there, away at the back, in the gloom, which he'd never seen before, its sails stashed away. He stared at the faded red wood. He reached out to it, as it seemed to reach to him. Then he shook himself – a fog of memories lost.

He looked around the barn once more. No sign of Aunt Pen. Nothing. No sign of their adventure but for the holes in the roof and mess of debris on the dirt floor. No sign except one feather that clung to Jojo's sleeve.

It was a big feather. White, speckled with gold. It seemed to glow there in the sunlight. One feather. Jojo did not brush this away.

He plucked it from his arm and held it up to the light. The sun shone down through it.

Jojo stared at the sun and then looked back to the feather. His dad made her fly, that's what Mum said. She remembered that at least.

Jojo pocketed the feather. He'd need this feather. He did not know when or why. But he knew it. This feather was important. A first memory. A first feather. Something was happening here.

'Come on, Joey,' Ricco shouted.

Jojo took one more look at the boat, then at the sun and followed his grandad and his brother.

The rest of the day passed without any more happenings. Aunt Pen had up and vanished. No one except Jojo seemed to even notice though. Mum's burping had stopped, as the faerie had said it would. And they got fish and chips from Something Fishy in the village.

'Not as good if you're not on the beach though, is it,' said Grandma as if she'd forgotten that they didn't talk about the beach. Didn't go there and didn't talk about it and Jojo knew why now. It was a special place. Dad's special place. He knew that like he knew that memory was not imagined. He'd seen Dad again. His vanished dad was reappearing, was breaking into Jojo's mind. He just didn't know why. He was desperate to ask questions, but too anxious about the sad blank faces he'd get as a response.

No one spoke for a long while.

Until, 'They only use fresh from the sea at Something Fishy though,' said Grandad.

'Huh,' said Ricco, spluttering potato across the table. 'Chips come from the sea?'

Grandad shook his head. Jojo laughed.

'Fish, Ricco,' Mum said. 'Fish comes from the sea.'

'Ahhh yeah.'

'And the best fish,' Grandad went on, 'you get right here in Dor, of course.'

'He would always complain of the fish in London,' Mum said. She didn't look up from her fish and chips. Mum didn't say which 'he' she was talking about. They all knew. Maybe Mum was remembering too.

They ate quietly after that.

Dad going missing had always seemed like something that had happened to someone else, something in someone else's story. It was an idea of something that had happened. But now . . . now it was becoming real. Now it was becoming his story.

Now he had a dad. The man who called him buddy, taught him to skim stones. And . . . bought a barn . . . and . . . liked fresh fish! Jojo had a real memory. Memories were erupting into their lives. But it was more than just memories. It was a person. He knew, he just knew, that somewhere out there was a man who loved him. A real dad.

But where? Lost? Gone? Where?

Jojo looked at the faces around the table. Faces he loved. People he loved more than anything in this world. Yet he suddenly felt alone. Somehow he knew that whatever was going on with Aunt Pen and these reappearing memories, it was something he'd have to figure out alone.

He wondered why these memories had returned now. What did it mean? What could he and his dad have to do with magic and the darkness hanging over Elfhaeme? Where did Aunt Pen figure in all this? Where was she now? And what was it that she couldn't tell him? This was surely just the start of the story.

Sun and Moon

The sun set over the village of Dor and the moon rose. Night was the land of the Sandman and in the night he came. He moved as a shadow, edging round the pools of light which filled the main street. Near the station, he stopped and set his pitch-black eyes on a small house just off the main road.

He took specks of golden dust from that same bag attached to his belt. He let them tickle across his palm. Did he inspect them, muttering to himself? Or were those whispers for the specks themselves?

With a final word and a puff from the Sandman's lips, the specks lifted from his hand and began their spiralling journey. Up they went, following the cloaked figure's gaze to the window of the house, which was lit with the glow of a gentle night light. In they slipped through the narrowest of gaps, continuing their dance within. Its journey at an end, the dust fell on sleeping eyes – the eyes of Mr Terry Tanner, the town's taxi driver, and his wife Regina, who ran a hair salon in Upford.

And soon they dreamed. He of a brand-new car, a large black one with big wheels, which he drove up to London and around the streets while everyone looked on, amazed.

She dreamed of a holiday, of lying on a sunny beach.

The Sandman had not tarried. He slid along the high street, from dark to dark. And then he stopped again. He stopped outside a glass-fronted shop. It read *Clarkes and Clarkes* in big gold lettering. The Clarkes had been the town's book-keepers for as long as anyone could remember. Mr Clarke had taken over from his grandfather, who'd taken over from *his* grandfather, and so on. Right now though, it was the young Miss Cherish Clarke, twelve years old, that the Sandman was visiting.

He took a pinch and puffed and made her dream of pulling on her football boots and playing for England in the World Cup Final.

Further on and further out of town, until the Sandman stopped at the cottage of the Hayes family. Here he left dreams of outer space and flights amongst the stars for the eldest in the family, old Mr Hayes the dairy farmer.

There were many dreams that night in Dor before the Sandman made his final stop, in a field of wildflowers overlooking the furthest-flung cottage. The Lockes. Married to the Troughtons, the oldest of Dor's old families. The Troughtons had been visited by the Sandman in Dor for over three hundred years.

'Is that what *helping him* looks like to you?' said the Sandman.

At first it appeared he spoke to no one. No sound but the gentle chatter of piskies in their own language which even the Sandman could not understand. Nothing stirred beside a ripple in the wildflowers, pink and yellow and white, and the tall grass that surrounded him.

'Penperro . . . ? You are here?'

The meadow rippled again, seemed to shake itself and then a tiny figure rose from where she lay amongst the plants.

'I am here,' Penperro said. 'As you well know.'

'Well?' said the Sandman. He had not turned to look at the faerie, who was now seated on a rock beside him. Instead he stared down the slope to the one-storey cottage where the Locke boys slept, their mother and grandparents too.

'Hmmm?' replied Penperro. 'The boy has needed some . . . shaking.'

'Shaking?' said the man in black and you could be sure, beneath that black cloak, an eyebrow rose high in question. 'Your sister has done more than shaking. Your sister has wrought terrible magics. Your sister has—'

'. . . broken the very contract that holds the worlds together,' Penperro finished. 'I know this better than most. I've seen it.' Penperro's mind went back to that grey and empty land where she had taken Jojo. 'Everything has been lost to Mab's madness. Even my sisters are gone, lost and scattered. Even my own Aoede, the oldest of us all, the singer of the song, is gone to who-knows-where. I know what is at stake, Sandman.' Penperro's voice had risen, grown to something fierce and with it had risen a cloud of piskies, buzzing around her, their chatter become a hiss of anger. But then the faerie yawned and the piskies dropped back down to their flowerbed homes.

'You grow tired,' the Sandman said. Penperro had aged since last they spoke. Her hair was whiter. Her skin more wrinkled. She sat a little less straight. 'Do you have enough in you? Enough fire left?'

Penperro breathed in deep then sighed. 'I am tired,' she said. 'But I am not yet asleep, not like the boy. I know . . . I believe I know . . . what I am doing. He does not. Not yet. But all the fire that is left, I will place in his charge. Soon he will see. Soon he will act.'

The Sandman stood. 'Soon he must. He must see the path ahead. If he is to find the lost Locke, he must see the way and he must walk it. Hurry, Penperro.'

Penperro did not stand to join him. She dipped her head and sighed again. 'All you see are the things that will be, Sandman, master of dreams. You underestimate the knowledge of what has come before. To shape the present, you must first understand the past.'

But the Sandman was gone.

'Memories,' whispered Penperro, 'that's what the boy needs. He must know what he's lost before he knows what he wants.'

Mr Goodfellow

The next day, Jojo rose late. The rest of the house was in full swing, Grandad was back from his walk. Grandma was watching her work-out routine. She didn't actually do much of the routine but she liked to watch and move, even if just a little. And Trevor liked to watch Grandma.

Mum had gone to work. There was a note beside him on his pillow. Jojo read it, still lying in bed.

Sorry Jojo. Had to go early. Too much to do! So sorry I can't be there. I tried to wake you but you were fast asleep. Have a lovely day, sweetheart. I'll see you real soon.

Mum! She'd gone. No proper goodbye. The note shook a little in Jojo's hand. He really was alone.

And then he read the final line.

Aunt Pen says she'll take you out. Exciting!

Exciting? Exciting or terrifying?

And where was Aunt Pen?

Jojo sat up. He looked around the room. Ricco's sleeping bag was empty.

Where was Aunt Pen and where was Ricco? No! No! He

should have thought of this. He should have been up before Ricco. He had to protect him. Who knew what wishes Aunt Pen could be granting at that very moment?

Jojo dashed through the living room.

'Morning,' Grandad said, looking over his newspaper.

'And one and two,' Grandma said, slowly gyrating in time to the work-out routine.

'Morning,' Jojo called over his shoulder, as he burst into the kitchen.

He got one look at a grinning Aunt Pen as Ricco opened his mouth and said in a cheerful chirrup, 'I wish my dreams would come true.'

Jojo skidded to a halt, bumping the table, sending the salt shaker rocking and then rolling away. 'Oh no, Ricco. What have you done?!' he said.

Ricco just grinned at his brother as Aunt Pen wriggled her nose and blinked. There it was, that flash of light. And then . . .

Nothing.

Jojo held his breath.

'So?' said Ricco. 'What we waiting for?'

'Hmmm . . .' said Aunt Pen, looking at her hands, which seemed to wrinkle and crease before their eyes, light brown spots appearing on the dark packing-paper skin. What was happening to the faerie? Was she growing older? Did each wish age her just a little more? She looked up at Ricco. 'You see, it's not an exact science, this magic, more an art form. Never sure exactly what might happen.' She stuck a finger in her mouth, plucked it out and thrust it in the air like she was testing the wind. 'Something is happening. Somewhere. I guess we'll have to wait and see.'

Jojo took a breath and sighed. Then, 'Ricco?!' he said, looking crossly at his brother.

Ricco still grinned. 'Exciting, isn't it! This is gonna be amazing!'

'This is . . . this is . . .' said Jojo, shaking his head. 'I told you, she doesn't know what she's doing. You need to listen to me. This is gonna be terrible.'

'Nope,' said Ricco simply, his five-year-old head bobbing in excitement. 'This is gonna be the best.'

But it was neither terrible nor the best. In fact it was nothing at all. Nothing happened. Nothing happened at breakfast – just a normal breakfast of cereal and mugs of tea this time. Nothing happened when the boys got themselves ready. Nothing happened when Grandad announced after watching another rerun of *Mickey Mack's Family Game Show*: 'I hear you boys are out with Aunt Pen today. I'm taking Trevor for a walk, then I'll catch up with you later,' and off he went.

Even Jojo found himself somehow disappointed. He didn't want another burpfest and certainly not another fall from a great height. But when your faerie godmother casts a spell, you expect . . . well . . . something.

So when Aunt Pen said, 'I hear there's a very good park here in Dor,' Jojo and Ricco both looked at each other with expectation glinting in their eyes.

'Is this it?' said Ricco, running to the hall, plucking a football from the box of outdoor stuff and pulling on his shoes. Jojo followed slowly.

'Yes,' said Aunt Pen, 'this is our trip to the park.'

'But is this *it*?' said Ricco. Shoes were on. Laces being tied. Aunt Pen was pulling on her dark red coat with the gold buttons, making sure all her pendants were in place.

'Never know what you might need,' she muttered to herself.

'It is. I know it!' said Ricco.

'Ah, one more thing, I think,' said Aunt Pen and headed back into the house. The two brothers listened, standing in the hall, as Aunt Pen clattered around in the kitchen, bowls and tins bashing, crashing. What was she up to?

Jojo and Ricco looked at one another then ran back to the kitchen. They pulled the door open. There she was, the faerie godmother, twirling, whirring, back and forth, pulling, throwing, tasting. She was a blur, dashing from spot to spot. She was everywhere all at once.

Flour flew in the air. Sugar poured from a great height. Eggs were juggled and spun from one side of the kitchen to the other. Raisins seemed to fall like rain and bounce up from the floor like rubber balls.

Through it all you could hear Aunt Pen singing an indecipherable song of unknown words.

Ricco let out a laugh, *Ha!* And he was spinning on the spot, trying to take in the flurry of blurred cutlery, crockery and cascading ingredients.

Aunt Pen didn't slow down until she stopped with a *Ping!* and closed the lid on a cake tin. 'Just thought we might need a cake,' she said.

Jojo and Ricco's mouths fell open. They'd made their fair share of mess in their time. But this was something else. Every surface was covered in pans and packets. Every spot of floor was sprinkled with flour, raisins, sugar. Globs of butter seemed to be stuck to the ceiling.

'Oh, don't worry about that,' said Aunt Pen. 'Let's see. Let's see,' she said, feeling for another one of her necklaces. 'If we just . . .' Then she found the one she was looking for, a pendant in the shape of a sort of purse. 'This is it.'

She flicked the tiny bag open and pulled out, again, something too big to fit inside, something like the recorder that was currently back home on the chest of drawers in Ricco and Jojo's room, the instrument Jojo had never practised. Only this one was gnarled and wooden, like it had been grown on a plant rather than carved by hands.

She put it to her lips and blew. From under her curled fingers a tune escaped. Short and commanding, like a call or command. Then she waited.

'What are we waiting for now?' Jojo said. 'We need to get this mess cleared up.'

'Hold on,' said Aunt Pen. And waited some more with a finger in the air and an eyebrow raised.

'Get the dustpan and brush, Ricco,' said Jojo.

But then . . . *knock, knock, knock.* There was a knocking

somewhere. As if on a door. But this wasn't from back down the hallway at the front of the cottage. This was coming from somewhere in the kitchen.

Knock, knock, knock. Then a voice, 'Hello, anybody there?' A small voice, gruff and tinny like a swarm of bees.

'Ah, here we go,' said Aunt Pen, turning toward a high-up kitchen cupboard where they kept the tins of tomatoes and jars of jam and other things of that sort. She pulled it open to reveal a tiny man, seated on a pot of honey. His eyes were bright and twinkling like that of a young boy, but his face was aged and craggy, like Grandad's. He wore something like the clothing Jojo had seen the faerie version of Aunt Pen in, only his were all browns and greys. He was smaller than the faerie, yet taller than the piskies. He was the height of a school ruler.

'Mr Goodfellow,' said Aunt Pen.

'Oooh, lovely bit of baking,' said Grandma, who had entered the kitchen on silent slippered feet and was looking at the incredible mess with a small smile on her lips.

'At your service,' said the tiny man. 'Good afternoon,' he said, raising his little hat to Jojo. ''Ello,' he said, winking at Ricco. 'Charmed,' he said, with a small bow to Grandma. 'You may call me Hob.'

'What a delightful man,' said Grandma. 'Are you here to check the meter?'

Jojo and Ricco was lost in silence again.

'Very good, Mr Goodfellow. Did you have far to come?' said Aunt Pen.

69

'Not at all, not at all. Just servicing a rather nice house in Upford. All done. Spick and span as usual.'

'Wonderful,' said Aunt Pen. 'Well, just a little job here. Kitchen needs a tiny spruce.'

Jojo, with his mouth wide again, managed to shake himself back to life: 'A tiny spruce! This place is an absolute mess. How can this . . . this . . . I don't know . . . are you a faerie too? How can *he* get all this sorted?'

'I beg your pardon,' said the tiny man, getting up from the honey jar, looking back at it, then with one swift movement, spiriting it away inside his brown tunic. 'I am no such thing. You people! Think you know everything. You know nothing. I, as anyone in Old Albion could tell you, am a goblin. Absolutely finest cleaners, sorters, neateners, declutterers, ship-shape-makers, orderfiers and organisers in all the world. Thank you very much.' With this he lifted his chin and turned to Aunt Pen. 'Just the kitchen, faerie?'

'Just the kitchen. Well . . . maybe you could fix Mrs Locke a little lunch too.'

'Oooh, wonderful,' said Grandma. 'Cheese on toast, please.'

The goblin, Hob or Mr Goodfellow as Aunt Pen had called him, gave another little bow. 'I would be most honoured to serve lunch to so fine a lady. If you would care to take a seat.'

Grandma bustled past the two boys still crowded in the doorway. 'A delightful man,' she said. 'Just delightful.'

The goblin leaped from the cupboard, flipped, twisted and landed with a roll amongst the flour and raisins on the floor. 'I'll begin here, I believe,' he said, and proceeded to pull a large dustpan and brush from within his clothing. 'I'll take my payment where I find it,' he added.

'Of course, of course,' said Aunt Pen, pointing the boys out of the kitchen and snatching up the cake tin from the egg-and butter-smeared table. 'Let's leave Mr Goodfellow to it.'

'We can't just—' started Jojo.

'We can,' said Aunt Pen as the door swung shut behind them.

'The kitchen—' tried Jojo.

'Will be spotless when we return,' said Aunt Pen as she hustled them into the hallway.

'But Grandma—'

'Is in excellent hands. She'll have the best cheese on toast of her life. Goblins, as well as being excellent cleaners, happen to also be very fine chefs.'

And with that Jojo, Ricco and Aunt Pen were out of the door and on the way to the park.

'That was awesome,' said Ricco.

'It rather was, wasn't it,' said Aunt Pen, grinning her usual mischievous grin and heading out into the world.

Lost in the Park

The park was busy. There were littler kids than Jojo all over the playground, which looked out towards the hills around Dor. Ricco, still clinging onto the football he'd brought, ran off to climb the big netting pyramid. Jojo scanned the slide, zipline, climbing frame and settled on a sulky swing. Aunt Pen watched on from a bench like she was just an ordinary aunt taking her nephews to the park.

How could Mum and Grandad and Grandma all believe that she was their godmother? Even though they'd never, never seen her before. Must be magic. Bad magic? Maybe she wasn't here for good. Maybe she was here for bad.

Jojo sat on the swing, his legs dangling, his face pointing away from the hills. He knew if he swung high, you could catch a sliver of the sea beyond the village. He didn't swing high though. He was too busy thinking.

Aunt Pen seemed to be asleep on the bench. Ricco had made some friends at the top of the pyramid – Ricco was like that. They were seeing how high they could jump from it.

Maybe Jojo should be taking advantage of this whole thing. If she was his faerie godmother then what should he be wishing for? If Jojo could wish for anything, if he was going to use Penperro's magic, what would he wish for? Riches? Adventures?

Finally Jojo kicked off from the ground. Swinging his legs back and forth. He was flying then. Not real flying, not like the day before.

He wondered, staring up at the sky, falling back down to the ground again, and again and again, if he should phone Mum to tell her about who Aunt Pen really was. But he knew, he just knew, that it would sound even stranger over the phone, all this magical madness. Grandad? Maybe he should tell Grandad? What would he say? How would he even begin?

Sky. Swing. Ground. Swing.

And would he believe him? *Could* he believe him?

Ground. Swing. Sky. Swing. Ricco. Ground. Swing. Ricco. Sky.

'Jojo,' Ricco shouted. 'Let's play football.'

Jojo slowed and then jumped from the swing, not twisting and flipping like the little goblin but still being rather pleased with his landing.

'Yes!' said Ricco. 'Good one.' Then as they walked towards Aunt Pen on her bench by the gate: 'It's not happening. You said something was happening. Where's my wish?'

Jojo had been thinking about this all the way to the park. Something was happening, Aunt Pen had said. But nothing. Not yet.

'I don't know, Ricco. But maybe it's a good thing. I told you about the castle and the throne room and the . . . and the . . . faeries.' He had told him about it on the way to the park, with Aunt Pen chipping in corrections and alterations.

He'd told him about the flight through space and time, the thrones, the statues and the darkness. He'd told him what he'd wished, for Mum to stay home, and what Aunt Pen, or the magic in her, had done.

'Who knows what your wish will turn into. Who knows what dream she'll pick?'

'What?'

'Well you said you want your dreams to come true. You didn't say *what* dream. You've got to be specific . . . I think.'

'You think?'

'Ooooh, football,' said Aunt Pen, rising from her bench. 'I love football. One of the best, I am.'

They played football on the big field where the woodland started. You could walk that woodland all the way along the river which ran from Upford to Dor – Jojo knew that because they'd done it with Grandad. It was Grandad's favourite walk. He liked to walk from here to the faerie mounds. A clump of little hills on the edge of Upford, which legend said were the ancient homes of faeries. Each was topped with a ring of stones, bedded in the ground. Grandad went there a lot. He said they were important but could never say why. He just knew it.

What had Aunt Pen said about faerie mounds? They were the way into her world. You just needed to walk around them in a storm. Jojo would not be doing *that* in a hurry. The sight of that dark land filled his thoughts and filled him with fear. Especially the throne room. What did it mean? Why had they flown there? Why there? Why him? It seemed so unreal in the middle of the day in the park.

Little did Jojo know, this was also the woodland where Dad had grown up, building dens, climbing trees, finding animal burrows and camping out at night to try to spot the creatures. Grandad had not told them, because Grandad, like Jojo, had a big empty space where his son should be.

Aunt Pen fiddled around with her necklaces then found one that impossibly contained a portable football goal: she pulled it out of a tiny pendant like a magician pulling out infinite handkerchiefs and swapped it for the cake tin. Jojo kept looking round to check no one was watching. They didn't seem to be.

Aunt Pen plonked the goal down in front of the thick trees.

And then they played. Aunt Pen really was rather good. She was a good bit better than Ricco and Jojo, at least. And Ricco was good. Like, really good. He was six years younger than Jojo, but better than him already. Even Jojo knew that. Aunt Pen, though, was even better.

They played knockouts. First Aunt Pen beat Ricco, dancing round him, slotting the ball through Jojo's legs into the goal. Then Aunt Pen beat Jojo, with a mazey run around a family picnic; she flicked it over a dog and, catching the ball on the volley, sent it rocketing past Ricco.

A girl called Cherish asked to join them. She was small but whippet-quick and older than Jojo.

They made Aunt Pen go in goal. But even with three of them working together, they couldn't put anything past her. To Jojo, to Cherish, to Ricco, back to Cherish. Whack! Dive! Save!

Cherish laughed, 'Your grandma's really good!'

'She's not our–' began Ricco.

'She's our aunt,' said Jojo.

'Thank you very much,' said Aunt Pen, bowing. 'As good as you may be one day, Cherish Clarke.'

The girl blushed, gulped and frowned all in one.

Jojo looked from one to other. What did Aunt Pen know? He didn't ask. How much would Aunt Pen say if they let her?

'Come on,' Jojo said. 'We can beat her.'

But they couldn't.

It was strange to see this old lady leaping one way, springing the other, rolling, twisting, beating the ball away, in her big skirt and necklaces and coat. People had stopped to watch, cheering as this old auntie flew around the park.

Jojo, Ricco and Cherish were gasping and sweating but Aunt Pen was fresh as a daisy.

'Come on, you three,' she shouted after she'd yeeted the ball halfway across the park. 'You gotta have more than that!'

Ricco looked at Jojo. 'Penalties?' he said.

Jojo nodded.

'We're gonna take penalties,' Ricco shouted back to Aunt Pen, then trotted off to retrieve the ball.

'Right you are,' she said.

Ricco took the first one. Hard and fast toward the bottom corner. Aunt Pen dove and caught it in one curled hand.

Cherish next. She tried the other corner. The same result.

Jojo booted it straight down the middle. Aunt Pen punched it away with a growl of victory. Then a laugh.

'National Five-Aside Champions we were, me and my sisters. A long time ago.'

Sisters? She'd mentioned her sisters before. But it was now that Jojo thought how remarkable this was. She had her own family somewhere. A family of faeries. He wondered if they were close. If they got together for holidays and Christmas and stuff.

Penalty after penalty, Aunt Pen just caught them or swatted them away like they were flies. There were more cheers for their faerie godmother. And she enjoyed every one. Raising her fists in the air, she grinned to the small crowd of picnickers and dog walkers and teenagers who'd given up their game of frisbee.

Ricco had given up too and was sat in a little heap of boy by the goalposts.

'Right,' said Cherish. 'This is it.' She planted the ball on the spot. She took a big run-up. The crowd started a slow clap, getting faster and faster as Cherish approached the ball. She swung and smacked it. It soared, spinning in an arc away from the goalie, toward the top right corner. It was going in. *Surely* this one. You've never seen a penalty like it.

Jojo stood and stared. This was it . . . and then . . . like a cat, Aunt Pen pounced. Her arm seemed to stretch. Jojo could have sworn she gave a little nose wriggle, an imperceptible blink. Her hand shot out like a bullet. Her fingers clawed.

One finger, the longest, grew a little longer and caught the ball at the very last moment, sending it spiralling past the post.

The crowd groaned. No goal. Then cheered. What a save!

'Oh, come on!' muttered Jojo. No goals and the ball was gone, somewhere into the woods behind.

Ricco leaped up. 'I'll get it!' and off he ran.

'Good effort,' Aunt Pen called to Cherish.

'Oh no,' said the girl, her eyes on her watch. 'Oh no. Have you seen the time? I've gotta go.' Then she turned and ran. 'Sorry,' she called over her shoulder. 'Sorry about the ball! If I've lost your ball, I'll replace it!'

'Don't worry!' Jojo called, then half waved and walked over to where Aunt Pen stood in goal.

'Did you see where it went?' Ricco was shouting from the edge of the woods. 'I can't see it.'

Aunt Pen was grinning from ear to ear. 'I am rather good, aren't I?'

Jojo stuck out his tongue. And laughed. 'It must be around there, buddy. Right where you are,' he called to Ricco.

Ricco stepped further into the stand of trees. Further in, further away from Aunt Pen and Jojo.

The crowd had all left, returning to dogs and towels and

78

their abandoned frisbee, not bothering to watch a boy searching around for his lost ball.

'Nothing!' shouted Ricco.

'Hmmmm, mysterious,' said Aunt Pen.

Jojo took a puff on his inhaler and looked up at her. 'What have you done?'

'Me? Me? I don't do anything. Only what you ask. Your wish is my command,' she said, looking down at Jojo then doing a funny little bow.

'I can't seeeeeeeeeee . . .' shouted Ricco. Then silence.

Aunt Pen and Jojo spun, their eyes searching the woods, leaping from tree to tree. Empty. No Ricco. He was gone.

'What have you done?!' said Jojo again. 'What have you done?!' Then he was off, running toward the trees.

'Hold on,' said Aunt Pen and she was with him, running.

'If some other strange creature has got him . . . or if you've sent him off to some place . . . or if he's got some terrible illness too . . .' Jojo didn't stop to say any of this to Aunt Pen, he just shouted it over his shoulder as they ran straight into the woods.

'He was around about here,' said Aunt Pen. They crashed through the trees to the spot where he'd been.

'He's not here!'

'Hmmmm, very strange.'

'It's more than strange,' said Jojo, pushing forward into the woods. He couldn't lose another part of his family. He just couldn't. 'It's an absolute disahhhhhhhhh—'

Then he too disappeared.

'Well. At least we now know what happened to Ricco,' said Aunt Pen, staring down into a deep, dark hole in the ground.

She held her nose, closed her eyes and stepped off the edge, following them down, down, down to who knows where.

Voices in the Dark

'Dark in here, isn't it?' said Penperro to the dark.

And the dark answered: 'It's really dark.'

'Oooo,' said Aunt Pen, feigned surprise in her voice. 'Who's there?'

'What do you mean, who's there?' said the dark. 'It's me.'

Aunt Pen didn't answer for a few moments. She thought about who this could be, here in the dark. 'Are you my conscience?' she whispered.

'What?' said the dark. 'It's me. It's Jojo. You came down right on top of me. It's amazing you didn't break something. You're very light.'

Aunt Pen was quiet a few moments more. 'A bit disappointing really,' she said, 'I'd quite like to meet my conscience. She's got a few things to answer for, truth be told. So, where are we?'

'Where *are* we?' said the dark, who was doing a convincing Jojo impression by worrying about everything.

'How should I know?' said Aunt Pen. 'This isn't even my world. This is *your* world. Tell me, what would a big hole be doing here, do you think? What was it Ricco wished for . . .'

'. . . his dreams to come true,' Jojo whispered. But what did Ricco dream of?

It was Jojo's turn to think for a moment, listening to the

rustle, clinks and clunks as Aunt Pen fiddled with her necklaces. He thought about the things that lived in the dark – moles, mice, rabbits . . . rats! Was this a dream or a nightmare?

'This is a rather big tunnel,' said Aunt Pen. 'You know what they say . . .'

Jojo did *not* know what they say. There was a click and light shone out from a table lamp that Aunt Pen held in her hands – a normal sort of table lamp with a wire and plug on the end, but this wire went trailing back and into one of the bags that hung around the faerie Aunt Pen's neck. No wonder she was so light. She was back to her tiny faerie form.

'They say, *big tunnel, big monster.*'

Jojo looked around. It really was a big tunnel, almost big enough for him to stand up in. The walls were hard-packed earth, as was the ceiling and floor. There, lying on the floor was the football. No sign of his brother. What *had* Ricco been dreaming of? For surely this was the dream he had wished for. Visions of giant mutant rats sprang to Jojo's mind. 'Ricco?' he shouted.

'Oooh, I wouldn't shout,' said the faerie. 'Big monsters don't like people shouting after they burst through their front doors.'

Jojo threw up his hands. 'Well, what are we supposed to do?' he said.

'Mmmmm,' said the faerie, licking her lips. 'Do you smell that?'

'What?' Jojo sniffed the air. There *was* a smell. Not unpleasant. Familiar, almost wafting above the smell of wet earth. It smelled like toast.

'This way,' said Aunt Pen. 'I'm hungry.'

'What about Ricco?'

'Yes, yes, I mean, let's find Ricco.' Then much more quietly, as if Jojo couldn't hear her there in the silent tunnel, 'But if there's a meal to be found then so be it.'

The table lamp lit the way along the tunnel as Aunt Pen went first, casting long shadows up and round the walls. Aunt Pen was singing softly as they stepped, as quietly as they could toward whatever awaited. This time, Jojo could make out what she was singing:

> *'We're gonna get you, giant monster.*
> *We're gonna get you, giant monster.*
> *We're gonna get you, giant monster.*
> *Unless you get us first!'*

'Shhhhh,' said Jojo. 'You're really not helping.'

Was the lamp getting brighter or was there a source ahead, lighting their way?

'Sometimes you have to help yourself,' whispered Aunt Pen, and then too quietly for Jojo to hear, 'And sometime soon, Jojo Locke, you will have to do precisely that. And you will find, as you're finding now, that beneath the worry and questions there's a seed of bravery.'

There *was* a light ahead, glowing round a bend in the tunnel. And it definitely smelled of toast – toast and hot chocolate.

And what was that? Voices?

'Shhh. Stop,' said Jojo. 'What's that? Is it Ricco? Monsters don't talk, right?'

Aunt Pen had stopped. She cupped a tiny hand round her pointed ear. 'All the best monsters talk,' she said.

Jojo hesitated. What was round that next bend, in that warm glow? There was definitely more than one voice. And what was that? Laughter? How many creatures were there? He had to get Ricco, though. He couldn't let one of Aunt Pen's magic wishes devour his little brother. He just couldn't. He hurried past Aunt Pen. 'Come on,' he whispered. 'Quickly.'

'There you go,' whispered Aunt Pen.

'And quietly!' hissed Jojo.

The faerie dropped her voice to a breath. 'Courage will be needed.'

So they stepped slower than ever toward the light and the voices. The bend was running out. And they could hear what was being said now.

'Oooh, we're gonna eat them all up,' said one.

'Yum, yum, yum,' said another.

'Do we really have to wait for the others?' said a third. 'Can't we just get started?'

Jojo gulped. He could see it now in his mind: some terrible monsters, all ratty and sinister, sharp teeth and vicious claws

84

holding his brother, waiting for him and Aunt Pen, waiting to gobble them up.

What kind of dreams had Jojo been having?

'Come on, Jojo,' he said to himself. He just wished he had something to fight with, a stick or a bat or something.

Aunt Pen tapped him on the shoulder. 'Here. Take this.' She handed him the table lamp. Jojo took it in one hand and raised the other to question what on earth Aunt Pen expected him to do with a pink lamp with a tasselled fringe. Aunt Pen mimed a downward whack and a thrust as if she had handed him a sword.

Jojo shrugged. It was better than nothing, he guessed. He gripped the lamp in both hands, swallowed, breathed out and took the final few steps round the bend and into the glow.

'Hey!' said one voice.

'Our guests,' said another.

'Jojo!' said a third.

Jojo dropped the lamp and dropped his jaw. It took a few moments to take in what he was seeing in the rather nice room in front of him. A big, round table, piled high with sandwiches, cooling toast, pots of tea and hot chocolate, plates of cakes, biscuits and cream-filled puddings.

Seated at the table were three huge badgers. And at the far end was Ricco, grinning from ear to ear.

'Aha. We were beginning to worry about you,' said the largest of the badgers, wearing a pair of round glasses and a fluffy red sweater. If Jojo had to guess, he'd have said she was the mum. But there was no time to make guesses as two paws took his hands.

Each paw belonged to two more badgers, much smaller badgers.

'Come on *den*,' said one, in the voice of a tiny girl.

'Do it *den*, come and sit down,' said the other.

Jojo, as stunned as he had been at any time in the last few days, followed the badgers to a very snug cushioned seat at the table.

'Ah, of course,' said Aunt Pen, vanishing the lamp and finding her own chair, 'Badgers. Big badgers. Not monsters after all.' She grinned and winked at Jojo.

'Aunt Pen?' said Ricco. 'You *are* a faerie! This is like . . . like my actual real dream.'

'Cake,' said Aunt Pen, conjuring the fruitcake she'd made earlier that day from one of her many bags and parcels. 'I told you we'd need this. You can't turn up to a badgers' tea party without a cake.'

'A cake!' said the largest badger, the mum, taking the cake from Aunt Pen. 'How wonderful.'

'You knew about this, didn't you?' said Jojo.

'Well . . .' said Aunt Pen.

'You knew all along?'

'Well . . .'

'What was all that about monsters?'

'Made it exciting, didn't it?! And now we know.'

'Know what?'

'What dreams are made of.'

Jojo frowned. What did that mean?

'OK,' said the mum badger, 'I think we can start!'

'Yeah!' said the gathered badgers. 'Time to start.'

Aunt Pen whispered to herself once more: 'Ready for a real rescue mission.'

A badgers' tea party is a busy affair. The two brothers, Bobby and Buddy, seated either side of Ricco, grabbed and snuffled and scoffed at marmalade on toast and cucumber sandwiches and scones with cream and strawberries. The twin sisters, Coco and Ottie, the littlest badgers who had led Jojo to the table, helped themselves to piles of blackberries, crumpets dripping with butter and jam, and big slices of fruit cake. Ricco was just as quick as the badgers. He tried a bit of everything: egg sandwiches and raspberry roly-poly, honey on toasted muffins and chocolate eclairs, scones and cakes and puddings. Jojo hesitated at first – this magic business was just a little too much – but his hunger soon got the better of him and he had a sandwich and another and another, each filled with some curious meaty paste.

'Oooooh,' said the mum badger, who was busy pouring everyone tea and hot chocolate, which was then passed round and round the table, 'I didn't know you humans liked earthworm paste sandwiches. Quite delicious, aren't they?'

Jojo coughed on his mouthful, and, not wanting to be rude, swallowed slowly. After that he stuck to the cake Aunt Pen had made – which, he would tell you now, was the finest, most buttery, most delicate, light and airy, rich and fruity cake he had ever had.

Aunt Pen kept taking slices of bread to the fire which roared in the corner and crisping them until dark, dark brown, just before they burned. Then she'd return, slather them in butter with a sprinkle of salt and crunch her way through.

The talk was of the kind that is had over a big meal:

'Oooh, this is delicious.'

'Have you tried this?'

'Mmm-nyumm-nyumm, scones!'

And Mrs Badger sometimes said things like, 'Bobby, one slice in your mouth at a time please,' while Bobby tried to shovel a third or fourth piece of chocolate swiss roll into his mouth, or, 'Coco, would you please stop dipping your paws in the cream!' while Coco and her sister each had a bowl of cream that they were happily eating by hand.

It was the finest, funnest, homeliest tea party JoJo could imagine. Looking at Ricco's glowing eyes, alight with contentment, he could see it really was a dream come true.

Mr Badger

Soon, the party slowed down. Aunt Pen sat smiling contentedly at Jojo and Ricco. Ricco was so full he could only sip at his chocolate. Jojo had abandoned his third slice of fruit cake half eaten on his plate. Ottie and Coco were making finger paintings with jam on their plates and even the badger boys had grown full, or full enough that they were now only nibbling at slices of flapjack.

'Now,' said Mrs Badger, who it seemed had not eaten anything, only busied around, pouring drinks, piling cakes onto others' plates. 'Now that the tea party is almost over, I think we should have a few toasts, don't you? I did have a bottle of something fizzy somewhere.'

She looked across the destruction in front of her, plates of crumbs and piles of crusts, empty trays and cups. Buddy burped and looked embarrassed. Something glassy clinked under his chair. Mrs Badger scowled and opened her mouth.

'No, no. Not to worry. Allow me,' said Aunt Pen, still in faerie form. She reached for the packages slung about her, rummaged for a moment, pushing aside canvas bags and brown boxes, before delving into what looked like a small picnic hamper. Finally, with a flourish, she produced an impossibly big bottle of golden, shining, bubbling liquid.

The cork popped as she pulled it out and liquid fizzed and steamed over the top.

'Tintinhull cider,' said Aunt Pen. 'Fresh and fizzy. You won't find a finer drink outside of Kernow.'

With the help of Bobby and Buddy, whose mouths were still full, Mrs Badger fetched glasses. Between them they had them filled and distributed to the whole party.

'Can I start the toasts?' said Bobby.

'Certainly,' said his mother.

'To the lady over there who brought the cake,' he shouted, pointing to Aunt Pen.

'To the lady over there!' shouted all the badgers and Ricco, who was right into the swing of things.

Jojo said, 'To Aunt Pen.'

Aunt Pen herself seemed to blush. She stood and bowed a little nod of a bow as glasses clinked and everyone had their first sip of the fizzy apple drink, which really was the most refreshing, most fizzy, most richly apple-flavoured thing any of them had had. It took them a few moments to all comment on how wonderful the drink was before Buddy shouted over the party.

'Me next,' he called, swallowing a final mouthful of flapjack. 'To Mum, for all the rest of the food. It was great, Mum.'

'To Mum,' everyone shouted, even Jojo, and they clinked and took another sip. The drink really was delicious and was perfectly capping off all the fine food.

'Me, me,' squeaked Coco. 'To the biscuits. I liked the biscuits.'

'And the berries,' said her sister.

They hadn't quite got the idea of toasts, but still the whole party raised their glasses and repeated, 'To the biscuits and the berries,' before clinking and sipping.

'I have a final toast,' said Mrs Badger. 'But before then, would any of our guests like to raise their glasses?'

Ricco was giggling with Bobby, who had just shoved another pawful of strawberries in his mouth.

'I will,' said Jojo. He lifted his glass and said, 'To Ricco and Aunt Pen for bringing us here. It really was quite fun.'

'To fun,' everyone shouted. Clinked and drunk. Ricco grinned at his brother. Aunt Pen winked.

When it fell silent, Mrs Badger cleared her throat. 'So to our final toast. I would like us to raise our glasses to Mr Badger.' At this, she looked to a corner of the room that neither Jojo nor Ricco had paid much mind to, where the biggest badger of the lot lay on a long bed. His black fur seemed even blacker than his family's and where the white stood out on his chest and streaked on his head, it seemed even whiter. His chest rose and fell, occasionally he snuffled. He was absolutely fast asleep.

And with that one glance, a memory came to Jojo. It came to him as the other had, out of a clear blue sky. It broke into his mind, or more accurately, *out* of his mind, out of wherever it had been hiding.

Memories were breaking out.

He remembered in that moment, another party, in another place.

Jojo was wearing a party hat, a pointy fabric thing, with a gold star on the front. He knew right then that his grandma had made it. Did she make things? Did she? He was five years old.

The table, like the one in the badgers' sett, had been laden with food but was now a mess of crumbs and empty plates.

He remembered most of all his dad, asleep on the sofa. He remembered them all laughing at him.

'Leave him be,' Mum said. Her stomach was round. Ricco was on his way. 'He's working hard. Saving up for the big move. Soon, Jojo, we'll be in our new house, just across the road from Grandad and Grandma's.'

But Jojo didn't leave him be. He ran and jumped onto the chest of the man on the sofa. His father. His dad.

'Oomph,' said his dad. He opened one eye. He grinned. 'Buddy!'

Arms encircled the five-year-old Jojo.

That's what he remembered. And with that, tears sprang to his eyes.

'Are you OK, young man?' said a kindly voice. Mrs Badger.

Everyone stared at Jojo. They waited for him. How long had he sat there, staring at Mr Badger? Jojo coughed and took one more look over at the hairy creature on the bed.

Above the bed where he lay, there was a painting, dark with shadow. Jojo squinted to make it out. A woman, it seemed, small and pale with dark red hair and deep black eyes.

'I'm OK,' said Jojo. 'I'm OK.'

'OK, sweetheart,' Mrs Badger said. 'I'll finish my toast

then. To Mr Badger. He really is the finest man, and our family would be incomplete without him.'

'And Gurt,' squeaked Coco.

At the end of the bed lay a big, shiny black woodlouse, the size of a dog, who at the sound of her name shook herself awake.

'And Gurt,' repeated their mum.

They raised their glasses again for the final toast, a solemn toast this time, with heads bowed. 'To Dad and Gurt.'

At the sound of her name again, the woodlouse made a croaking noise, like a bark. And as if in answer, the painting above the sofa began to move. Jojo was sure of it. Eyes moved in that dark face. They flicked around the room before settling on Jojo and Ricco. Anger, blazing anger, filled those eyes and the red hair grew somehow redder.

'You're right, Gurt,' said Mrs Badger. 'It really is time Dad was waking up. Bobby, give him a little shake.'

Jojo could not take his eyes from the painting. Even as Aunt Pen said, 'I think it might be time for us too.'

Bobby was at his father's shoulder. He shook him and as he did, the ground around them shook. Eyes glared. Hair blazed. And the ground shook.

'Woah,' said Ricco.

Mrs Badger didn't seem to notice. None of the badgers did. 'Give him another little shake, Bobby.' The boy badger did and the ground now rocked and heaved back and forth. There was a deep grumbling from the ceiling above.

'Ah,' said Aunt Pen, 'it really is time for us to be going.'

'What's happening?' shouted Jojo, as the earth now roared and bits of dirt and rock began to fall from the cracking ceiling.

The badgers carried on as if nothing out of the ordinary was happening at all. Bobby and Buddy had begun to clear the table. Coco and Ottie were flicking globs of jam at each other.

'Run!' called Aunt Pen. 'My magic is only so strong now.'

With a sad look at the badgers they were leaving behind, Ricco vaulted the table and ran. It was clear now, they couldn't stay put. The ceiling was coming down in chunks and a great chasm was yawning open across the floor. Jojo took one more look at the dark painting. An arm seemed to be reaching out of it. He did not wait any longer to see. He kicked his chair back and hurtled after his brother and the shouting faerie.

'Run! Run!'

It was not easy staying on their feet as the world seemed to roll back and forth and the ground beneath them churned like the surface of a stormy sea. Ricco stumbled, but stayed upright, now neck and neck with Aunt Pen, who seemed to float above the rocking earth, dodging and ducking falling slabs of stone, holding aloft her table-lamp torch. Jojo was right behind them, pelting back along the fearful tunnel, away from the light of the badgers' home.

'Quick!' shouted Aunt Pen, looking back over one shoulder at Jojo.

He looked up, he tried to call, 'I am going as quickly as I can,' but all he got out was, 'I aaahhh . . .' before he found himself face down on the frenzied ground. His foot was burning. He'd stubbed it against something. He scrabbled to stand, reaching back for the something that had tripped him. A rock, the size of his fist. On impulse he seized it and held it tight in one hand, feeling its smooth surface, feeling the hole in the centre of it. A strange rock. Back up, he ran on, pocketing the stone.

He couldn't see Ricco and Aunt Pen now, it was grown almost pitch dark. He couldn't see the ceiling falling in, but he could feel it, dirt and pebbles raining over him.

'There's no way out,' shouted Ricco from some way further on. 'It's blocked.'

Jojo's breath was gone. His heart was pounding. But he didn't stop. He shouted, 'Aunt Pen, get us out of here. Make us fly!'

Then there was a light. It didn't come from a lamp or a fire. It came from Aunt Pen herself. She shone in the dark. 'Reach for me, Jojo! We have to be touching, Ricco.'

With his last breath of musty underground air, and his last burst through the falling rocks, Jojo launched himself forward, and clung, fingertip to fingertip, to his faerie godmother, while from the other side Ricco leaped and took hold of her ankle with a clawing hand.

She blinked, she wrinkled her nose and they were gone. They were light, bursting through the dark, they plunged on, bouncing from crumbling ceiling to cracked floor. Finding their way blocked, the light bounced back and shot through cracks and crevices, sliding forward. Like a whisper, like a razor, they passed through the most minute fissures, the tiniest rifts, till without sound they burst out into the daylight.

Then . . . *SPLASH!*

They were no longer light. They were themselves. They were there in the real world, struggling for breath, struggling out of the water they'd landed in.

Ricco! Ricco couldn't swim!

Jojo broke the surface as someone leaped from the bank into the water. A huge man with curly grey hair and skin just darker than Jojo's. He saw the old man reach Ricco, grab him and pull him toward the bank. Jojo swam the few strokes and pushed out of the water, joining Aunt Pen, the auntie Aunt Pen. Ricco and the man soon scrabbled out beside them, coughing and spluttering.

And there they stood, dripping, panting, gasping, covered in dirt, smeared with mud, bruised and shaking. They were not in the park any longer. They stood clinging to one another on a grassy path, in a woodland, beside a river.

'What . . . where . . . ?' said a voice that came from the man who'd rescued Ricco.

'Arf, arf,' barked a dog that stood beside him and farted gently – *Pppftt.*

'Errrrm . . . Grandad,' said Ricco.

Jojo reached into his pocket, past the round stone, to his

asthma pump. He took a deep breath and a puff. His lungs loosened. He glanced at the river behind them. At Grandad. He opened his mouth. What was there to say? How to explain them all appearing as if by magic and falling from mid-air into the river?

He didn't need to explain. Aunt Pen spoke first.

'So,' she said, pulling a pair of spectacles that Jojo had not seen before from one of her many pouches, and placing them before her squinting eyes, 'I'm a faerie.' With a wrinkle of her nose and a blink, a breeze rushed from a long, tube-shaped pendant on her neck, like a minute trumpet. The breeze whirled around them, got in under their clothes, whistled through their hair and dried them all in moments.

'Ahhh,' said Grandad, feeling his dry clothes. His eyes widened, taking in his grandsons, who nodded at him, looking both as guilty and alive as he'd ever seen them. 'Well, that does explain things, doesn't it.'

And the Rocks Break

I would take you there, but there we must not stay,
I would take you there, but it is not for us, the land of fae,
Soon we must return, or in Dinn Ainnhir we will sleep,
We must awake or be forever lost, sunk unto the deep

In that castle on the rock, in a western corner of Elfhaeme, the ground also shook. The ground shook. The rocks shook. The foundations of that ancient fortress shook. The House of the Nine rumbled and groaned.

Memory broke out.

Deep inside that citadel, a man lay asleep on a white bed. Old, he seemed, bearded and dark. He slept a sleep that had gone on too long. A sleep which must come to an end or be the ending of all things.

It was from here that memory broke out.

Beside the bed in which the man slept, a woman sat. Her hair was white, but with a hint of the red it had once been. There was little to see of her. Her head was in her hands.

The shaking continued, it shook the inhabitants of that room. The shaking grew. Groans from the deep. And then a crack and a boom. Somewhere in the deep, rocks broke.

Memories broke out.

Explanations

After a sip of Kernowan Moonshine to warm them all, Grandad said, 'Well, I think a few more words could go toward that explanation.'

So he got a few more words.

As they walked back home, trying with very little success to dust themselves off, Jojo and Ricco told their grandad the story so far of flights through space and time, of near-death falls, of Mum's mysterious burping and of the trip underground to visit badgers. They told it well with only the occasional interruption from Aunt Pen of, 'Well . . . it's not quite that simple,' or, 'It wasn't exactly like that,' and, 'There's a bit more to the whole adventure than they're letting on.'

They spoke about the tunnels collapsing, about their escape through the dark. Jojo showed them all the stone with the hole in it that he'd picked up.

'That's called a hagstone, that is,' said Grandad. 'It's meant to be magical.' He glanced at Aunt Pen, frowned. 'Maybe it is? They say it shows the world how it really is.'

Aunt Pen did not comment on the stone but gave Jojo a meaningful look. Perhaps she was saying, *That's important.* Or, *Keep that safe.*

Jojo frowned at it. Peered for a moment through the hole. And with a shrug, dropped it into his jeans pocket.

It was not until they turned onto the lane that they finished with how they flew as light through the cracks in the earth.

'And that's when we landed in the river,' Ricco said.

Grandad stopped there on the street, lost in thought for a moment. To Jojo, there seemed to be the merest hint of a tear forming in his eye.

'I know what you're gonna ask,' said Aunt Pen.

Grandad swallowed something stuck in his throat, words or thoughts or those gathering tears. 'Do you now?' he said in his gruff way.

'I do,' said Aunt Pen. 'And I can't do it.'

To the brothers it was like eavesdropping on one of those adult conversations where two people speak in riddles and half-finished thoughts.

'You can't?' said Grandad. 'Or *won't*? Is it possible?'

Aunt Pen peered deep into Grandad's eyes as Grandad stared right back. Jojo and Ricco looked back and forth between the pair of them. '*I* can't do what you would ask,' she said. 'There are certain constraints on my magic. Certain limitations on all magic. And that, Mr Locke, is at the heart of the problem. More needs to be fixed than one lost son. But if that *were* fixed . . .'

Grandad took a long, long breath and let out a sigh that seemed to deflate his whole body, like he was a bouncy castle with the pump turned off. His eyes fell to the pavement.

'*I* can't do what you would ask,' Aunt Pen repeated, reaching out and lifting Grandad's chin with one finger, as you would do to a young child. In that moment, Jojo saw Aunt Pen in a whole new light, not as a tiny faerie, not as the rather odd aunt, but as someone or something ancient and knowing – a faerie godmother true. 'But something can be done about what you would ask.'

Grandad swallowed again. He fixed her with a stare again. He went to speak. But the faerie spoke first.

'However, before you ask, I cannot even say what must be done or will be done. There's a bigger plan at work here, Mr Locke, and we are at a tipping point. If we were to take one misstep, we'd fall. If I were to push too hard one way or another, we'd fall. If I were even to open my mouth and speak of it, it'd be the end. Much would be lost for ever. There is so much I cannot speak of. I am bound by the same magic that imprisons . . .' Her words stopped. 'So much I cannot say.'

Grandad stared a moment more, then said, 'I think I need some more fresh air,' so he and Trevor kept on walking. Jojo and Ricco were left to ponder the conversation as they made their way along the final stretch of the lane.

Back inside, there was no sign of the strange little man Hob Goodfellow, whom they'd left Grandma with. But neither was there any sign of the colossal mess Aunt Pen had left in the kitchen. Grandma was happily knitting.

There was no sign of Aunt Pen either. They did not know at what point in those final steps she had slipped away but she had. Again, she was gone.

After the events of that afternoon, the boys owed themselves a quiet afternoon. They changed out of their filthy clothes and Jojo shoved them into the washing machine. With many words of thanks for 'just the greatest day', Ricco plonked himself in front of the television.

Jojo couldn't concentrate though. Not even on everyone's favourite programme – *Mickey Mack's Family Game Show* – *coming to you live each and every day.*

Now he knew what Grandad wanted, his mind was a-whirr. He wanted his missing son back. He wanted that empty space in his head, in his heart, in their homes to be filled.

Jojo knew all about that empty space. The space that was now filling, tiny bit by tiny bit. Memory by memory.

He could feel his father now. Feel his arms around him. He knew what it felt like to have him, to be held.

There were tears in Jojo's eyes, as he sat there watching the Thorpe family compete for the grand prize of a holiday in Florida. He was glad no one turned to look at him. No one saw the tear run down his face and onto his thin pyjama top.

He missed his dad. For the first time ever, he missed his dad.

And he knew Ricco felt something the same. What did he dream of? Family? Sure, a family of badgers, but still family.

Jojo found himself feeling slightly guilty, guilty that he hadn't thought to ask before for the one thing that everyone in his family needed. An end to the emptiness.

An answer to the mystery of the missing dad.

Guilty, but he knew that before these days of magic had begun, he didn't even know it was what they wanted or needed. Not really. Now he knew it, right in his gut.

They needed the wrong made right.

What had Aunt Pen said, the same sort of thing she'd said to him about limitations, constraints on her magic? Not everything was possible. She couldn't do what Grandad wanted.

I *can't do what you would ask*. That's what she'd said.

When Grandad returned, Jojo did not lift his head to meet his gaze. And Grandad sat heavily, not rising for some time even when Trevor parked himself on Grandad's lap, which he hated.

Mum rang in to a very strange atmosphere.

'Hello, darlings,' she said, her face appearing on Jojo's phone – they got reception by holding the phone half out of the window.

'Hey!' Ricco fizzed. 'We had the best day!'

'Wow,' said Mum. 'That's great. With Aunt Pen?'

'Yeah,' said Ricco.

'Hey, darling,' Mum said to Jojo, who tried to turn his frown into a grin.

'Hey,' he said.

'So what did you get up to?'

'Well—' began Ricco.

'Nothing,' said Jojo quickly. What was the good in Mum knowing? He couldn't tell her now. They couldn't tell her there was a faerie who could grant wishes but the one wish that should be made, could not be made. He couldn't tell her that.

Now it was Mum's turn to frown.

'It was the best day, but you did nothing?' she said.

'They went to the park,' said Grandad, appearing just in time to lean over Jojo's shoulder and appear in the little box that showed what Mum saw on the other end of the line. 'And then the river.'

Well, that was true, thought Jojo.

'Fun,' said Mum.

'And a very nice little man made me lunch,' said Grandma, now appearing at Ricco's shoulder. 'Little Goodfellow.'

Grandad glanced over at his wife. He hadn't heard this bit.

'Erm . . .' Mum said. 'That's nice. Is Aunt Pen there? Pen? Pen? Did they behave themselves?'

But Aunt Pen was still nowhere to be found.

That night, once again, Jojo could not sleep. One thing Aunt Pen had said ran round and round his mind. Not a storm of thoughts this night, just one, again and again, hitting him from all angles. A thought without an answer.

Something can be done about what you would ask.

That's what Aunt Pen had said. How? What could be done? What should be asked? What should be wished for?

There's a bigger plan at work here.

The same cryptic words she'd said to Jojo in his bedroom.

He dreamed that night of Mr Badger asleep on the sofa, watched over by that woman with the red hair – a terrible, fearful woman. Her eyes blazed even in his dream.

The words of Mrs Badger rang out, '*It really is time Dad was waking up*,' and somewhere far away a drum was playing or a clock was ticking.

Time was running out.

The Man in the Moon

This, by chance, was exactly what a certain starry-eyed, black-cloaked man was saying to the faerie Penperro on a grassy sand dune overlooking the beach of Dor.

'Time is running out,' said the Sandman, all in black, the stars in his eyes grown dim.

Penperro held an hourglass balanced in one hand. But instead of sand pouring through and filling the bottom half of the glass phial, one minuscule feather floated downward, more slowly than possible, to join a pile of hundreds of the same.

'The seeds have been sown. I have done what needs be done. All he requires now is a push. He must know what is within him: courage – the will to act,' she said.

The moon shone across the sandy beach and glinted on the rippling waves. It was a calm night. As calm as any you could wish for. But the king of dreams and the faerie godmother did not look to be enjoying it.

'They will come here soon,' the Sandman said. 'They must.'

Out at sea, the moon's rays caught on a strange series of waves.

'Dolphins,' he said. 'A whole pod. Maybe a dozen of them. They're making their choice – this side or the other. If we fail, the gate will close. There will be no travel between our world and this one. All magic will spill from the human world too as it does from Elfhaeme. No more dreams. No more moonlight. No more dust motes dancing on a ray of sun.'

As the Sandman spoke, Penperro lifted her eyes to look round to their right to a huge rocky arch stretching out from the cliffs into the wash of the waves. *The gate will close.*

Penperro looked up to the moon. It was empty tonight, no man looked down; for the man in the moon was sitting beside her on the sandy dunes with a bag full of stardust and words of warning. He'd make no rounds tonight; he'd set no dreams running through the minds of mortals. All his mind was now bent on their great task.

'I know what happens,' Penperro said. 'All magic. Gone. Elfhaeme will fall. My sister will fall too along with all of us. I do not believe she knows of the danger. And I cannot get to her to tell her now. The ways are closed even to me.'

'And would she listen, if you could?' said the Sandman.

Penperro sighed. A deep sigh. 'She did not. When I warned against loving a mortal man, long years ago, she did not listen. Maybe I should have . . .'

'The past has been and gone,' said the man in black. 'It will not come again.'

'Perhaps not,' said Aunt Pen. 'Perhaps though,' her voice dropped now to the faintest of whispers, 'we can shape a new past.'

They looked together out at the beach. 'You cannot hold it back much longer. You must show him more.'

Penperro vanished the hourglass into a locket which looked exactly like a pocket watch on a chain.

'Well then,' she said, 'I will.'

The Beach in the Bathroom

Jojo had slept, eventually, with that thought ticking always in his mind. He'd slept and slept long, throwing off the running and digging and madness of the day before.

He knew nothing of the conversations the faerie had had with the Sandman. He did not see clearly what she was steering him towards. He only knew that whatever she was up to, it was unpredictable and wild.

Jojo woke to a whispered conversation in the hall outside his door.

'I want to see him,' said Grandad. 'Even if it is just one last time.'

It was quiet for a moment but for the tinkling of pendants and lockets. Jojo pushed his blankets down, sat up and listened hard. 'That can be done,' said Aunt Pen.

'How?' asked Grandad.

'Make a wish. What do you want to see?' said Aunt Pen.

'Well . . . it's difficult,' muttered Grandad as Jojo shook the sleep from his head and began to take in what he was hearing. 'There's so much . . . so much I can't remember. I . . . I—'

'How about,' said the faerie, 'how about the day you taught him to fish?'

Jojo leaped from the bed. 'Grandad,' he called, running for the door. 'Don't do it.'

But he was too late.

'Mmm ... yes ... I wish to see my boy on the day he learned to fish.'

Jojo pulled the door open as that flash of light pulsed from Aunt Pen. 'Oh no,' he hissed and squeezed his eyes shut. He got ready to make a grab for a hand hold, ready to plunge into water, ready for giant creatures to be all around him.

But nothing happened.

He opened one eye and looked up at Grandad, dressed in his coat and boots and Aunt Pen wearing a kitchen apron, staring down at him where he was curled on the floor. 'You OK, boy?' said Grandad.

Aunt Pen winked, the wrinkles around her eyes growing in length and depth as she did so. 'Breakfast,' she said, hobbling off to the kitchen with a cough.

'What have you done, Grandad? It goes wrong. It always goes wrong. She doesn't know what she's doing.'

But all Grandad said was another, 'Mmmm,' a deep rumble from his huge chest, as he hung up his coat. Then he made his way round to the kitchen with a, 'We'll see, won't we.'

*

Ricco was up, playing Jenga with Grandma. Grandma loved Jenga, the toppling tower game, even though her hands shook like they were tied to heavy weights.

In the kitchen, Grandad was at the table, which was spread with toast and butter, honey and jam. Aunt Pen was at the cooker, frying something. Jojo sat as she turned with a plate of puffed pancake-like pockets of gold.

'Oh yes,' Grandad said. 'Fry bakes. Pass 'em here.'

Breakfast went on without event. Grandad fed Grandma mini pancakes with honey. Ricco had thick slices of toast and peanut butter. Jojo, however, could not eat. There was a deep knot in his stomach. Something was coming again. Magic was on its way.

He kept his eyes on Aunt Pen who, he was sure, was ignoring him. Someone else was there too. No one was paying him any mind, but out of the corner of his eye, Jojo caught sight of Hob Goodfellow, tidying this, moving that. Jojo could not look right at him, no matter how hard he tried; his eyes seemed to slide off the little man and focus on something just to the left or right. But he was there, just out of sight.

Jojo wondered if he'd had enough of magic altogether. Enough of all this mystery. Enough of strange creatures and unknown designs. He wanted to know, for certain, what must be done. He'd ask. Soon, he'd make the faerie talk.

'Tinkle time,' said Ricco, standing and heading to the bathroom.

Jojo reached for a pancake and popped it in his mouth. Now Grandad had made his own wish. What would it bring? What day were they heading for?

'Woah-ho-HO!' shouted Ricco from the bathroom. 'You have got to see this.'

'Ah,' said Aunt Pen.

'What's up with you now?' said Grandad.

'Here we go again,' said Jojo.

'Oooh, Mr Goodfellow is back,' said Grandma.

Everyone apart from Grandma and the goblin crowded out of the kitchen, across the living room and down the hall to where Ricco stood beside the open bathroom door.

Ricco stared and gulped. As they approached him, water sprayed out of the bathroom door, soaking his pyjamas.

'Woah!' he said again, shaking himself like a dog, as Trevor the actual dog came bounding past them and through the open door.

'Trevor!' shouted Ricco and plunged after him.

'Ricco!' called Jojo. He didn't run after his brother. Not straight away. He stood and stared and took a deep breath.

That wasn't their bathroom in there. It wasn't any room at all.

Instead of the yellow and cream lino floor, a rocky slab sloped away down towards a swirling sea. There was no sink, no bath, no toilet, no walls. There was just the sea, and above, the blue sky, peppered with wisps of white cloud.

Jojo turned back to the hallway. Then back to the bathroom door and the sea beyond. He pinched himself again. No. He wasn't dreaming. There was a whole sea in his bathroom.

Ricco and Trevor had vanished from sight.

'This is the day,' whispered Grandad. 'I know it. I can feel it.'

'Come on,' said Aunt Pen. 'After him. You can't let him get lost in the past. We'll never get him back. He'll come back through tomorrow aged thirty years!'

The waves rolled in, sending another spray of spume. This time across all three of them. They shook, like Ricco had done and then as one leaped forward through the entrance, onto the rocks.

'Ahh. This is it. Trestle Beach,' Grandad sighed as the cool sea breeze hit them.

And it was the beach, Jojo could see, the beach not far from the cottage in the lane. The beach he'd seen from high in the sky. The beach that was imprinted in his mind. The rocks were at one end. To their left, sand and stones ran away in a long curve till they reached rolling sand dunes at the other end and then a huge stone arch beyond that, out at sea.

But it was not the beach. There was no ice cream parlour like Jojo had heard was there nowadays. (And maybe, in some fleeting memory, could picture – pink-and-white striped parasols, a giant whippy cone with a flake. He could almost taste the ice-cream.) On this beach there was just a line of old beach huts. *Lost in the past*, Aunt Pen had said. Jojo knew where they were but not *when* they were.

Across the beach, Ricco chased Trevor, laughing and leaping, still wearing his pyjamas.

'This won't do, will it?' said Aunt Pen. She wrinkled her nose, blinked and in a flash of light, all were dressed for a day at the beach. Jojo looked from Ricco's shorts and sandals to his own. Not just shorts, swimming shorts.

Aunt Pen looked unsteady on her feet for a moment. 'Jojo,' she said and reached out a hand. Jojo had seen this gesture before, from Grandma. He put out his arm to let Aunt Pen steady herself on him.

She was definitely ageing. Before their eyes, the ancient faerie was growing ever older.

Jojo looked from his faerie godmother out across the beach.

They were not alone on the beach. There was a couple strolling toward them, a group sat with their backs to the dunes, a man walking a dog, clouds of smoke escaping from around his head. None of them seemed to notice the door, standing open on the rocks.

'Ricco,' Jojo called. 'Come back.'

'If ever I heard something silly shouted, it was that,' said Aunt Pen. 'Might as well try to call the moon into your pocket as call your brother back from running around on the sand.'

'But you said—'

'I know what I said. But we can see him now. He isn't going anywhere, is he? Let him have some fun. And we can—'

Aunt Pen had stopped. Not because Jojo had interrupted her in return. But because Grandad was now heading out

114

across the sands too. Not toward the sea. Not toward Ricco. But toward two figures picking their way down the beach, pulling a red boat on some sort of trailer.

'Oh,' said Aunt Pen, 'I think this is what we're here for.'

'Is that . . .' Jojo whispered, for he didn't seem able to catch his breath. 'Is that . . . is that my dad?'

The Girl with Red Hair

'Wait,' called Aunt Pen. Not after Ricco. She wasn't worried about him, running, whooping, dancing with Trevor around his ankles. She called after Grandad. She called and she chased after him, hobbling along, dragging Jojo with her.

'Mr Locke,' she said, catching up, Jojo at her side without an answer to his question. 'You need to understand some things.'

It had been a long time since Jojo had been on that beach. But the sand beneath his feet – Jojo remembered that sensation somehow, the way it shifted, the way it moved.

'Listen to me, Mr Locke.'

Grandad didn't slow. He kept on walking, not running, but walking with purpose toward the two figures who were still making their way down the beach toward the sea, pulling the red boat, which now they were closer, Jojo could see was bigger than he'd first imagined and was held on a two-wheeled trailer contraption. They weren't the only ones heading for the pair: a girl, whose curled red hair flew out behind her, ran to catch them.

'Stop right there, Josephus Locke. Stop right there,' Aunt Pen said, forcefully now. Forcefully enough that Grandad did pause, a stone's throw from where the man and boy and boat would pass. Grandad didn't look back but looked down.

He waited a moment for Aunt Pen and Jojo to catch up. 'I've not seen my son for a long time,' he said. 'I intend to see him today.'

'You can see him,' said Aunt Pen. 'But please stop and listen to me for a moment.'

Grandad didn't turn. But he didn't start walking either. Not yet.

'We're in the past here. We're a long way from home. This is your past. Now think back. Think about this day. Do you remember having a chat with an older version of yourself, thirty years ago? Do you remember a faerie in the shape of an ageing human? Do you remember meeting your grandsons? Did any of that happen?'

Grandad stood statue-still. Jojo thought he understood what Aunt Pen was getting at.

'None of that happened. So now we're here you can't do anything that didn't happen. You just can't.'

'What if we do?' said Jojo.

'Well . . .' Aunt Pen said. 'You just can't. The world would reject us. We'd be spat back into our own time as fast as you can say *Merlin's beard*.'

'But I don't remember an old man standing here, watching us. Or a boy chasing a dog,' said Grandad quietly. 'None of us were there. This didn't happen.'

'But it did,' said Aunt Pen. 'It had to have. You can change time. Small things, like who was standing on a beach on a certain day. It's happening right now as we walk and talk and breathe, it's happening. And it already happened. But if you change big things – like talking to a past version of yourself. Well . . that's a big old time-travelling monster of a headache kind-of-complicated. The world would not be happy.'

Neither Grandad nor Jojo replied for a moment. What was there to say to that? But then Grandad, still quiet, still not looking back, said: 'So, I don't remember us being here and—'

'No. You don't. And we are going to keep it that way. We are just some ordinary people on the beach. OK?'

'Ordinary people on the beach,' said Grandad. 'So I can't—'

'No,' said Aunt Pen.

'And I can't—'

'I am sorry,' said the faerie godmother.

'But what if I—'

'Then we'd be gone. Back to the present day. Back to where we belong.'

'Where we belong,' said Grandad, setting out again, but not along the beach as he had been, not toward the figures, the man, the boy and the red-haired girl, whose voices now drifted across the flat sand.

'Will we catch anything?' said the voice of a boy. A voice which sounded a lot like Ricco's.

'You'll never find it, you know,' said the red-haired girl, as if she was having an entirely different conversation.

Grandad walked toward the sea, keeping his distance but

keeping pace with the man, who Jojo could see was Grandad. It was him. Not 'looked a bit like him'. It *was* him, just smoother, less grey, but the same golden brown skin. The same broad shoulders and straight back. A slimmer Grandad. A younger Grandad.

The wind caught his words and washed away his reply to the boy who walked on the other side, out of sight of Jojo. Younger Grandad and the boy Dad did not seem to notice them following along at all, but the girl had turned to look from where she trailed behind, one hand resting on the very back of the boat. She glanced at them, frowned then turned away, her eyes back on Jojo's dad.

They caught the boy's reply. 'And how will we know where to fish?'

Jojo wondered if his grandad – the man who walked just ahead of him, the old man who he didn't really know, who wandered along lonely rivers – missed all this. None of them came to the beach any more. Not since . . .

Did Grandad miss the sea and the sand and pulling a boat down the beach? Could the old man in front of him still pull a boat down a beach? It looked heavy. That boat. *That boat.* Jojo had seen that boat before – back in the barn, dusty and faded, but the same boat.

'We'll know,' said the younger Grandad. Their paths were closing in; they were closer now. Soon they'd pass Ricco where he was fighting Trevor for a thick whitish plank of wood. 'The sea's in our blood, you know. We're sailors, us

Lockes. Always have been. Right the way back to Josiah Locke. He was a pirate, you know. We've been seafarers since he sailed out of St Kitts three hundred years ago.'

Those words hit Jojo in the gut. He'd heard them before. Almost word for word. He'd heard his grandad say them on this same beach. With this same boat.

He was sitting in the boat that time though. He was sitting as his father pulled it down the beach. He remembered when he learned to sail.

When he learned to sail?

The younger Grandad sounded proud. Proud of who he was. Of where they'd come from.

'Will I be a sailor?' said the boy on the other side of the younger Grandad.

'I'm gonna be a sailor,' said Jojo in his memory.

'You can be whatever you want to be,' said the younger Grandad.

'You can be whatever you want to be,' said his dad in that memory that wound itself round this one.

Then the girl with red hair spoke, bringing him crashing back to the present, or the past, or wherever it was they were. 'You wouldn't find it if I gave you a thousand years,' she said. 'No one can find it. Don't you want to play?'

Jojo stopped in his tracks. Tears were welling up from that empty place that was filling again, filling with memory.

'Come on,' said Aunt Pen. 'No time for that.'

Jojo gulped and walked on. No time for that. He needed time, though. Time to think. Why were all these memories coming to him now? What did they have to do with the appearance of Aunt Pen? And who . . . who was this girl with red hair? He'd seen those eyes, that hair before too.

Jojo pushed down the thoughts. They would have to wait.

They followed the younger Grandad and the boy who was Jojo and Ricco's dad down to the sea. They stood and watched as man and son unloaded the boat from the trailer. They watched as the pair slid the boat across the wet sand and into the wash. They watched in silence out of the corners of their eyes, pretending instead to be looking out to sea.

All the while, memory came flooding into Jojo's mind like the crashing waves.

He'd done this more than once. He'd done this many times, been out to sea, in a boat with his father and Grandad. He just knew it. He could see it. He could see them laughing and smiling. He could see his dad, a dark silhouette against the moon.

He remembered sitting in that same boat, his father's arms around him, with the stars above.

He remembered.

Back on that beach in the past, the girl stood and watched too, her hands in the pockets of her floral dress, her feet making shapes in the wet sand.

Ricco and Trevor joined them.

'Woohoo. This is brilliant,' said Ricco, breaking their silent stare. 'And it's all in the bathroom? What we looking at?'

'That boy,' said Jojo. 'It's . . . he's . . . our dad.'

The boy in question had his back to the watchers. He had

not been much help to Grandad, the younger version, as the boat was rolled and dragged. And now he too watched as Grandad fitted a mast and sails to the red vessel.

'What?' gasped Ricco. 'Our what?'

The little girl turned at the noise and frowned at the group of Jojo, Ricco, Grandad, Aunt Pen and Trevor. But the younger Grandad and boy Dad were engrossed in the boat.

'Shhhh! They can't see us.'

'You mean like we're invisible?'

'They mustn't see us,' Aunt Pen hissed, still leaning on Jojo's arm. 'If they do, we'll be ejected out of the world and back to ours. It won't be much of a fun trip, I assure you.'

Ricco huffed then said, 'So is this like . . .' he looked around them. '. . . the past? Like we time travelled? Like in a film or something?'

Jojo nodded. Aunt Pen said, 'Well, it's a complicated matter. Listen . . .'

But before she could explain, a shrill voice broke the air, an angry voice, a voice that seemed bigger than the tiny girl who made it.

'What about our game?!' she shouted above the waves.

They were in the boat now, younger Grandad and the boy Dad. 'I'm going fishing, Mabel. Keep your game!'

'Who's the girl, Grandad?' said Ricco.

But Grandad didn't answer.

'Grandad? Grandad? Are you OK?'

Grandad looked away for a moment from his former self

and his son. When he looked back at Ricco, his cheeks were damp and water filled his eyes.

'I've not seen him in . . . so long. But this feels like it was yesterday. I remember it all. I remember his big hands, like yours, Jojo. I remember how excited he was about everything, just like you, Ricco. I remember . . . I remember how it felt to hold him. I can still smell his hair,' he said. 'I didn't think I'd ever remember again.'

Jojo knew exactly what he meant.

He remembered too. Big hands. How it felt to hold him. The smell of his hair. He remembered it all.

Jojo stepped towards his grandad, leaving Aunt Pen to totter on the shore, and pulled him into a hug. 'Grandad,' he said. Ricco joined them. So did Trevor, sitting himself on Grandad's feet. Over the breeze and waves they heard the unmistakable sound of the little dog farting.

Lockes at Sea

They hugged a while and when they turned back to the sea and to Dad and the younger Grandad, the red boat was fifty metres out amongst the waves.

'He showed me the world, your dad. When I was with him, it was like seeing through a pair of new eyes.' Grandad sniffed. 'I'm glad I'm here with you two. Remembering.'

There were just two figures in the boat. The girl with the flaming hair had gone – not on the beach at all. Gone.

'Well,' said Grandad, taking a long sniff of the sea air. 'As we're here, on a beautiful day like today, we should see what can be done about you city boys getting a taste of the sea.'

On all their trips down to Dor, Grandad had never spoken like this. They'd not come near the beach. No sand. No sea.

And now . . . a taste of the sea. Jojo didn't like to tell him that he already had. In his mind. He remembered it all. He remembered the sea and the waves and the feeling of the deep beneath the boat. Grandad must not remember this part, as Jojo had not remembered it till now.

'Hmm, we don't have a boat of our own but—' said Grandad.

'Ah,' said Aunt Pen. 'That's not actually true.' She set to searching her necklaces and chains.

'You've got a boat?' shouted Ricco. 'Brilliant! Let's do it!'

'How could you—?' began Grandad but before he could finish:

'Aha! Here it is.' Aunt Pen held up a pendant that looked like a fat fish, it even glimmered as one, the sunlight glinting off its green, blue and purple scales. 'Now. There's a knack to opening this. If I just . . .' She ran a finger along the fish's shimmering side. '. . . it should . . .' And with that, the mouth of the fish sprang open and out flew a yellow pellet, like a medicine tablet. It flew. Aunt Pen didn't reach for it; she knew better than that.

But Ricco did. He flung out a hand, grasping at the spinning yellow tube, for now it was a tube, as big as one of Mum's lipsticks. Ricco did not catch it, but knocked it on, out of reach.

Next Jojo made a grab for it, as it grew and twisted. It was the size of a school dictionary, bright yellow and seemingly made from little planks of wood. Like his brother, Jojo did not get a hand on it, just a fingertip. For a moment it seemed to balance there, on the end of Jojo's finger. He made to flick it backwards, but instead flicked it on.

Which was probably a good thing, all told, as now it grew and grew. It was a box. It was a cushion. It was bigger and bigger. And whatever reflexes Grandad the Navy boxer had once had, they returned to him then; he stuck out his hand and grabbed hold of a rope which flailed free of the bulging, billowing yellow thing. Or maybe it had hold of *him*.

Grandad's feet left the sand and he joined the huge yellow

shape, now as big as an armchair, as it sailed through the air towards the waiting waves.

Jojo would later say it was hard to tell where Grandad stopped and the yellow thing began. They were a whirling mass of yellow wood and flailing ropes, swathes of white canvas and the occasional sighting of Grandad's shock of silver hair and brown skin.

Then, as quickly as it had begun, it came to a halt. There in front of them, bobbing on the sea just a few paces away was a yellow sailing boat, larger than the red one that had just set out. A sailing boat as clean and ship-shape as any boat you could imagine.

'The *Skath Melyn*,' said Aunt Pen. 'She's a beauty, isn't she? Family boat, she is. Built by one of my sisters, Polperra the young, Polperra the explorer.'

'Grandad?' called Jojo and Ricco, only half listening to Aunt Pen, but still struck by the idea that this faerie had a family.

'Oh yes. Good point,' she said. 'Where is your grandfather? Should have probably warned you as to what would happen. Mr Locke?'

From the boat came a groan and before they could stop him, Trevor was out amongst the waves, yapping and splashing at the yellow boat – the *Skath Melyn* – and at the groggy-looking Grandad who pulled himself up and looked over the side at them.

126

He gurgled as he held his dizzy head in his hands. 'Just ordinary people on the beach, you said.'

∗

After they'd laughed, after they'd splashed through the knee-high water and pushed the boat out deeper, after they'd leaped in to join the recovering Grandad and well-settled Aunt Pen, who'd explained that certain magical objects were designed to keep themselves hidden from unsuspecting eyes, like this miraculous boat and, even incredibly, the doorway on the cliffsides. 'But that took a might more magic than I had thought it would.' After all that, the Lockes went out to sea.

If you've not been in a little vessel, amongst the endless waves, on top of the vast, vast sea, it's hard to explain how it feels. You feel small, for a start. You know you are powerless against the great muscles of the ocean current. You feel free as well. For in every direction there is possibility. There are the open waves and the horizon and beyond that, well, who knows what – and that is precisely the point.

'It's a bit small, isn't it?' Jojo said, clinging onto the very narrow, very low bench that lined the sides of the boat.

'Well, it's not built for the likes of you, is it, you great hulking giant,' said Aunt Pen.

'A bit rocky,' Ricco muttered. He was beginning to turn a shade of green.

'You'll feel all righ' soon enough,' said Grandad. 'You

heard the man – me, I mean – us Lockes are sailors through and through. Got salt in our blood!'

And Grandad was right. After a few minutes of pitching waves, both Ricco's stomach and the swell settled down. Soon Ricco and Trevor were scrambling from side to side:

'This is brilliant!'

Paarpp!

'This is just amazing!'

Paaarrrppp!!

'We're at home, having breakfast, and then we're here. In the sea! In a boat! Brilliant!'

Paaaarrrrrrpppppp!!!

Jojo, however, was lost in thought, lost in the past. Not this past but his own. He was, it seemed, getting to know his father. And there on the boat, he remembered more.

He remembered the red boat. He remembered his father sanding and hammering and fixing it with Grandad one summer, while Jojo sat on the bench inside and ate ice cream. He remembered sailing to a secret cove and Dad diving for scallops. He remembered learning to fish.

His dad was behind him, his arms around him.

'Look, buddy. You just flick it.'

His dad's hands were over his as he held his rod. Together they flicked the line, the weight and hook out to sea.

'That's it, bud. That's it.'

A kiss landed on the top of Jojo's head.

He remembered.

When Aunt Pen produced impossible fishing rods from

another necklace and Grandad proceeded to hand them out, Jojo clung to his, resting his head against the cool metal pole.

'Fishing,' said Grandad, 'is the art of patience. You cast and you wait. You wait and you watch, and you feel. You feel the fish beneath us. Feel them take a nibble at the bait. Feel them have a sniff. Feel and wait. Wait till they've really got hold.'

Some way away, a red dot was set on the calm sea and Jojo could imagine a much younger Grandad giving much the same speech to another boy – a boy who was his dad.

'Then comes the skill. The skill of the reel. Reel him in. Reel him in.'

While he talked, Grandad was showing Ricco and Jojo around their rods. Ricco was all in. But Jojo just nodded, knowing that somewhere in his head he knew all of this already.

It was Aunt Pen who had manned the boat, sailing them out to sea. She was still the woman Aunt Pen, but there was more and more of the faerie about her. Somehow she'd changed into the red jacket, striped trousers and leather boots that she wore as a faerie. Her gold hoops and bandolier of chains swung and glimmered as she quickly took down the sails, rolling them up and catching them and tying them in an elaborate array of knots.

'Here looks like a good spot,' she called over the winds and the waves.

They were some way out. The beach was a stripe of dusty

yellow. The rocks were grey stones, small enough you could reach out and grab them. The arch, which Jojo could not help but lift his eyes to look at every so often, was a faerie-sized door sitting atop the sea. There was something about that archway. Jojo couldn't shake the feeling it was watching them.

Grandad showed Ricco how to cast his line out on the other side of the boat from Jojo. And Ricco was soon watching and waiting. Aunt Pen was lying back with her eyes closed, letting the sun beat down. Trevor had settled himself next to the faerie, his head resting on her leg. Jojo still clung to the fishing rod.

'You OK, boy?' called Grandad, attaching a little worm on the hook on his own line.

Where had the worms come from? Another of Aunt Pen's necklaces? What else did she have in there?

'Mmmm . . .' Jojo nodded.

'Al righ', lad.' Grandad turned back to his own rod and left Jojo to the gentle lapping of the waves, the up and down and up and down. Left him to his memories.

Knock.

Was that the knocking of the waves against the bottom of the boat?

Knock. Knock.

No one else seemed to have noticed it. Ricco and Grandad stayed on the other side, staring into the water. Aunt Pen had fallen asleep.

Knock. Knock. Knock.

It was definitely coming from below. From Jojo's side of the boat. What would be knocking on a boat from the sea below? Jojo did not like to think.

Jojo leaned towards the edge of the boat. His stomach churned. His jaws tightened. He leaned further. He peered down into the sea.

At first there was nothing. There was reflected blue sky and reflected yellow wood. There was a dark shadow beneath the boat. Jojo was going to lean back. To think on these memories and what it all meant. But before he could, his eyes widened. There was something there.

Eyes staring back.

Two pairs of eyes. Huge eyes that grew larger as he stared. No, not larger. They grew closer. And Jojo could see more than just eyes – a nose on each of the two creatures, the small button nose of a child. And a mouth, wide, stretching, open, lined with sharp teeth. The last thing he saw was a series of pronged fins on top of the sea creatures' heads – a long fan of fin in green and purple and blue.

This was the last thing Jojo saw, because along with the strange faces, rose arms and hands. Hands with long webbed fingers which reached and grabbed and took hold of Jojo with an iron grip. Now he did call out.

'Grandad! Aunt P—'

He did not finish screaming Aunt Pen's name, for the creatures, small but far stronger than Jojo, pulled him from the boat, like you'd pull a fish from the sea. And with a splash, he was gone.

Trevor jumped up at all the noise, barking and farting.

Grandad dropped his pole and leaped, throwing out a hand to grab his grandson.

Ricco didn't know what to do. Something pulled at his fishing rod at that very moment. He held it in one hand and reached back with the other. 'Jojo!' he shouted.

Aunt Pen merely opened one eye, craned her neck to look. 'Mermen,' she muttered with a shake of her head.

Beneath the Waves

It was indeed a pair of mermen that had hold of Jojo. He struggled against their grip. He struggled and pulled. He wrenched at them. He twisted and tried to spin. He threw himself back and forth and back and forth.

Any minute, he thought, he'd be out of breath. Any moment, he'd simply drown and these things – these creatures? These children? They'd have him.

For children is exactly what they looked like to Jojo. Children smaller than Ricco. Five-year-olds? Like the children in the reception class at school. Tiny, fish-like children. Tiny, but strong.

They pulled him down and down as he struggled and struggled. Knowing at any moment his breath would fail. He was dead. This was the end.

Except it wasn't.

His breath was not running out. The surprise when he realised this was so great, that he forgot altogether about struggling.

He looked to the merboys. One looked back at him and . . . smiled? Was that toothy, stretched grimace a smile? That was definitely a wink.

Very strange – this sea creature had a bracelet on its wrist. Not some special twisted seaweed thing. A plastic band, green with algae, but unmistakably the sort of band put on you when you find yourself in hospital. But if one of these things had ever been in hospital, surely the whole world would know about it. Wouldn't they? Unless . . . unless . . . this thing was once a boy like him? Is that what they planned? To make him a fish-thing?

The merboy to Jojo's other side did not look at him, but peered onward, into the dark of the sea.

And here came Jojo's next great surprise. If he could look at the creatures and he could look ahead into the gloom, then . . . he could *see*, he could open his eyes in the salty water. And he didn't feel a thing – his eyes didn't sting at all.

Then he felt it.

Something had changed. In his neck. On his eyes. His hands too. He looked first to his hands where they were pulled forward by the fishchildren. His hands, green in the fading light from above, had grown webs like the creatures.

He couldn't see his neck, but looking sidelong at the merboys, he could guess what had happened. There, on their necks, as on his, were a series of slit-like openings. He knew what these were because of a particularly good school project on animal adaptation – these were gills, allowing him to breathe underwater. He couldn't guess what had happened to his eyes, but something had happened, something to protect them from the sea.

He screamed – it came out as a silent parade of bubbles.

Was he already changed? Was he a mer too? Would he be a sea creature for ever?

There was no way to ask. But he did have some hope. He was not scaled like the creatures yet. As far as he could feel, there was no fins on his head. He pressed his tongue against his teeth – no sharp little fish teeth.

More magic. Temporary like Aunt Pen's magic?

He had hope. And he took the hope with him, into the heart of the sea.

They did not seem now to be travelling altogether downward. They shot on, somewhere away from the boat. The fishchildren's long webbed feet beat at the water, propelling them as a trio of torpedoes.

Looking up and back, Jojo could see the sun – it was a pinpoint of light. But there was no sign of the boat. No sign of Grandad and Ricco and Aunt Pen.

Aunt Pen – would she come for him? Or was this her doing? He still wasn't sure if he could trust her.

He could see the seabed now, ripples of dark sand, gardens of waving seaweed. And fish – shoals of some little silver darting fish.

Onward they went.

Sand gave way to rocks. Fish gave way to crabs – bigger than Jojo would have guessed. Something else big was down there too. It moved out from behind a rock as they passed. A shark. Not huge like the films – but still a shark.

Jojo tried to shout again. To scream.

The merboys paid him no mind as they dragged him onward.

They were definitely not going down now. As the seabed sloped upward, so did they. More rock and weed, fish and crabs. No creature paid them any mind. The shark had not followed.

Ahead, now, Jojo could see an end. Ahead was a wall of rock, then a gap, then another wall of rock. They were not making for the gap. They were making for the wall. And they were not slowing.

Jojo pulled again. Pulled and tried to shout to the fishchildren. How could they not see it – the solid, dark rockface? Were they like birds, flying into a clear window?

Closer and closer they drew, and the rock grew darker, till it was a wall of black.

Jojo pulled and pulled but there was nothing he could do to get away from the mer. Their grip was iron.

Jojo screamed once more. Once more was all he had time for before they hit the black. But they did not hit a wall. Unseen to Jojo, they'd flown straight into the mouth of an underwater cave. A cave or tunnel, for as Jojo's eyes adjusted, he could see the smooth walls as they passed deeper into the dark, walls which began to glow.

Still they shot onward – these merboys were on a mischievous mission. They passed unseen through that dark tunnel and then, again, without warning, out into a large chamber, and out of the water, into the air. And there, finally, bobbing on the surface, the two merboys released Jojo's arms.

He sunk a moment, before kicking his own feet, kicking and swimming to the steps in front of him. When he reached them, he lay and drew in deep breaths. He rubbed his now sore wrists and looked around.

The chamber was not any old cave. This was in fact no cave at all. It was a room of sorts. It was circular, with large pillars holding up the ceiling above, which glittered with the light of thousands upon thousands of glow-worms. Between each pillar there was what seemed to be an arched doorway – nine, Jojo counted. But these went nowhere. Unlike the smooth, carved stone of the pillars and arches, the openings ended in rough, raw rock. There was no way out of the cave.

'Where on earth am I now?'

He said this to no one in particular, but as if in answer, one of the two merboys leaped from the water over Jojo, to the top of the steps. Here he pointed forward.

Jojo stood and clambered up the steps. They were slick with green weed and Jojo nearly slipped more than once. He joined the tiny fishchild at the top of the steps and took another look around.

He'd seen a room like this before. This one was smaller. But very much like the room he'd first seen the faerie Aunt Pen in, the room they'd travelled to by light. The room with the statues of a boy playing, a man standing in thought. The room with the two silver chairs. Although in this room, there were no stained-glass windows. And there were no silver chairs. Instead of the chairs was a wooden chest. The sort a pirate would keep his treasure in.

This chest is what the fishchild pointed to. He pointed and made to speak. But as with Jojo under the water, no sound came out. No words, but Jojo did not need them.

He could see what he'd been brought here for.

'So,' he said. 'Should I open it?'

The fishboy nodded. He reached out a hand to push Jojo forward. As the long, webbed hand came towards him, Jojo saw his own hands were no longer webbed. He felt his neck as the merboy nudged him – no gills. And, as he noticed this, drips of seawater fell into his eyes, stinging and blinding for a brief moment.

Phew! He was not a merman then. Just a boy in a cave. With no way out. No way out, but a way onwards.

He looked once more at the merchild. The creature nodded, pushed Jojo forward, then leaped away like a frog, back to where his partner waited, bobbing in the pool of water.

What was there to do?

Jojo walked on, leaving pools of water with every step as the sea drained from his clothes. He looked around at the empty arches and the shadows of the huge pillars. Shadows grew and shrank and grew again as the glow-worms moved and shifted above. He felt like he should be scared. But he was not. He felt like he was a braver boy than the Jojo Locke who had started this summer holiday.

It was a short walk to the chest. It should have been an old thing, Jojo thought, old and rusted, but it was not. The wood itself was shiny with varnish and the metal straps almost sparkled under the insects' light. Jojo could not imagine who had put it here, but it was clear it had not been here long.

Jojo did not hesitate. He lifted the lid.

As you or I would, Jojo expected this chest in this hidden room to be filled to the brim with treasure. He expected glittering gems, jewellery and piles of pirate plunder.

But, in this chest there was just one thing.

Now this thing *was* old. It was a coin. One, singular, nine-sided, red-gold coin. Jojo took it between finger and thumb. On one side was stamped a series of small symbols or maybe letters. Jojo spun it between his fingers. The other side depicted the head of a woman. A woman with curls of hair which caught the light and flickered red. But not just any woman. She had, without question, the pointed ears of a faerie. And a face that was instantly recognisable to Jojo.

And, as if in thinking of her, Aunt Pen chose that moment to appear.

The Peace of Mab

'What have you got there, Jojo Locke?'

Aunt Pen had not swum in. She had not been brought by scaly merboys.

Her voice came from high above. And as Jojo looked up to spy her sitting on some stone shelf near the top of those tall pillars amongst the many glow-worms, he held up the old coin. What was it doing here? Who'd built this strange place? He had no answers. But somehow, he knew this coin was important. He would need it. That's why he'd been brought here.

'A coin,' he said, 'with your face on it.'

What did it mean that this coin had Penperro's face on it?

'Not my face,' she said, still seated high up in the ceiling above. And then, in the next instant, with just a streak of light, she stood beside him, inspecting the coin. 'My sister's.' Another moment, another streak, and she was beside the steps leading down to the pool which Jojo had entered from.

'My sister ... the one who ...' Aunt Pen opened her mouth and closed it. Opened and closed. More lost words.

Jojo frowned at her, then down at the red coin.

'Keep it safe. It is vital. It is deathly important,' she said.

Jojo looked down at the chest. This chest for this one coin. Must be important. He pocketed the coin, deep into his shorts.

'What now?' said Jojo.

'Now,' said Aunt Pen, 'you act.'

'What?'

'Courage is not enough. You must have the will to act. And act quickly. Are you ready?'

'Ready?'

'Ready to RUN!'

And as she shouted this last word, somewhere in the rock below, a drum sounded. A thud that shook the floor and sent a ripple through that water where the merboys had been watching. They were gone now.

Jojo rubbed fresh drips of water from his eyes. He blinked and looked to Aunt Pen for answers. What was happening? What was this drumming that was sounding again?

But as he looked, she was a streak. A streak of light and she was gone.

'Aunt Pen?!' Jojo shouted as the drum beat again and the ground shook. Shook this time as if giant hands rocked the place. Jojo stumbled.

'How do I get out?' Jojo called, looking up at the ceiling where he saw what seemed to be, but couldn't be, stars going out. Glow-worms were one by one disappearing, crawling away or simply stopping their glow.

The earth drummed and the ground shook. Then there was a crack, like the bone of some huge beast breaking. This came from close by. From one of the rocky openings.

Jojo watched in horror as one of the craggy blank

rockfaces came to life. The rock shivered and rippled like the surface of the pool. It bulged outwards, taking shape. It was as if some creature pushed its way out of the earth and into the world.

Not any creature. A man. A huge man. From an entrance to Jojo's right came a great rock giant.

'AUNT PEN!' Jojo screamed again.

No reply except the earth pounding. No reply except another terrible crack and another and another, as each rock, one by one came to life, rippling as another stone-man pushed his way into the world. No reply except a grinding, crushing voice which came from the first stone-man.

'Who disturbs the peace of Mab?'

Jojo's mind raced. *Mab? Stone giants? A coin with a faerie's face? Abandoned by Aunt Pen? I'm ready? Ready for what? How will I get out? How will I get out? How will I get out?*

All of this flew through his mind as the stone-men took their first step into the world.

How would he get out? Only one way.

He ran to the pool as the darkness swelled. The frothing water caught the light of the last few glow-worms as they vanished. Caught the great shadows of the stone-men as they lunged forward.

Jojo plunged in. The darkness complete. The water now cold as ice.

'Who disturbs the peace of Mab?' came the voice again.

Jojo's body flinched away from the freezing water. His

142

brain said: 'You can't swim in this!' But his heart carried him in and on. And before he had time to decide, he was in the water and swimming. The water swirled and churned and threw him forward as a stone fist followed him in.

But he was gone back into the tunnel, pursued by the voice of the stone-man which dwindled to a bass thrum: 'Who disturbs the peace . . .'

There were no merboys now. No hands pulling him on. And no webbed hands and gills. Just his soft fleshy hands scratching against the rock walls as he swam and fought and pushed onwards.

'You won't make this,' his brain repeated again and again. 'Your asthma!' But what choice did he have? He swam on. He clawed at the walls and the water. He lungs grew tighter and tighter. There were no breaths to be had.

What was that ahead? Was that light he saw?

He'd read somewhere that when you died, you saw a light ahead. The light at the end of the tunnel. Was this it? Was this the end?

He swam on towards the light. His last strength. His last few strokes. And then, when he thought it was all he had, he found a scrap more, a little seed of fight still in his bones. A seed which grew and grew and burst out of him, pushing him through the final stretch into the light, out of the tunnel, into the sea and then up, up to the surface.

His first breath was like that gulp of cool water on the hottest day.

He lay, he floated, he gasped in all he could, while the sea washed around him.

He opened his eyes and he knew exactly where he was. There above him, a little to the left, was a huge arch; the waves crashed against it.

Safe, he thought. He could float. He could swim. He'd get back to the beach then he'd have some words with Aunt Pen. How could she leave him?

Safe, he thought. But then, above, a crack. Again, a great crack which seemed to echo off the waves. The arch itself was coming down. With another crack, a whole chunk of it splintered and shivered and began to loosen itself from the whole.

Then another sound turned Jojo. A voice floating across the sea. He crested a wave and saw the red of the boat as he heard the younger Grandad's voice.

'The Dor!' he shouted, 'It's coming down.'

The arch fell. Great chunks came crashing towards Jojo. He flung up his arms as if he could hold up the rock. But instead of being crushed, he found himself lifted.

He was sucked out of the water towards the beach as a huge jagged boulder fell right where he'd been.

He spun and turned as if he were caught in some invisible whirlwind.

'Jojo!' came a shout.

And there was Ricco and there was Grandad, and Trevor and Aunt Pen, all waving from a yellow boat which twisted and floated up into the air as if it too was in the tornado which pulled Jojo back towards the beach. Closer and closer they came together as they whipped towards the rocks.

And now the wind did howl around them.

'What's happening, now?' screamed Jojo. He'd had more than enough of this wish, of the past, of this little slice of magic.

'We're being ejected!' called Aunt Pen. 'We changed something.'

The wind was a roar now.

'The arch,' shouted Grandad. 'The Dor!' He looked back over the edge of the boat, which still spiralled through the air, turning round and round Jojo. Then Grandad let out a cry, a cry of pain, throwing his head into his hands. 'Arrgghh!'

'Grandad,' said Jojo.

At the same moment Trevor began to bark and Ricco called, 'That's the toilet door!'

Sure enough, hurtling towards them was their very own bathroom door. It wasn't fixed to the rocks on the beach. It too was caught up in its own tornado.

There was no time for any more talk as the chunk of wood plunged towards them. Only time for Jojo to grab hold of the boat. Only time to scream, which both boys did at the top of their lungs. Trevor barked, excitement not fear coming from the little dog.

Then the boat and the door collided with a splinter of wood and a final scream.

Out of the Storm

The wind had stopped. The screaming ended. Jojo could not hear the sea any longer. In fact, all they could hear was the familiar jingle of *Mickey Mack's Family Game Show*. Then Trevor started barking and his paws pattered away. Jojo opened his eyes.

He kneeled, panting, on the floor of their hallway. Beside him, Ricco was clapping and laughing, Grandad leaned against the wall wheezing, and Aunt Pen crouched to pick up a large strip of yellow wood from amongst the chips that covered the floor. The bathroom door stood open but beyond it was just their very ordinary pale cream bathroom. No sea. No waves. No rocks. Absolutely no merboys.

If Jojo had caught his breath, he would have been shouting at Aunt Pen – how could she leave him? But his breath did not come. He tried to stand, but his legs were like jelly. Instead he fumbled in his pocket for his waterlogged asthma pump.

'That was amazing!' shouted Ricco as Grandma appeared in the doorway to the living room.

'Now,' she said, 'I may be not certain of much these days, but I do know that something is not quite right here.'

'Erm . . .' said Ricco.

'Well . . .' said Aunt Pen.

But Grandad said, 'Come on, my dearest. I'll explain.'

✳

Grandad did his best to explain about the faerie and the wish and the day on the beach to Grandma, sitting on the sofa, once they'd all recovered and changed out of their wet and salty clothes. And, even though she didn't usually know Tuesday from Sunday, lost her glasses a dozen times a day and often put the dirty dishes in the fridge instead of the sink, she seemed after some time to have grasped Grandad's meaning.

'So, you're a faerie?' she said to Aunt Pen, who nodded and smiled, holding Grandma's hand tenderly, dark skin cupped around white. 'Well, that does explain that little fellow in the kitchen. He must be some sort of goblin type of a thing, correct?'

Hob Goodfellow, having already cleared up the mess of wood in the hallway, was at that moment busy in the kitchen, singing and trying to fix the washing machine.

Jojo stole guilty glances in his direction, still not sure if the broken appliance was down to his holey rock or not.

'Unsurprisingly, for so wise a lady,' said Aunt Pen, 'you are quite right.'

'Faeries and goblins and the like used to be quite common around here. Didn't they, Joey?'

Grandad nodded at this. 'That's what they say.'

'Remember that little girl,' Grandma went on. 'What was her name? Red hair?'

'Little Mabel?' said Grandad.

'Was it Mabel? They said she was more than half faerie. Remember?'

Grandad nodded again. 'They did. Strange little thing, she was.'

Jojo remembered the girl on the beach, remembered the red hair.

'Well,' said Grandma. 'I think it's past time I had a wish, then.'

'No, please, Grandma!' said Jojo, just as Ricco said, 'Yeah! Let's do it!'

'I think, I think,' called Jojo over his brother, 'I think she's gonna get us really hurt!'

Aunt Pen looked shocked as all eyes turned to her. But as Ricco and his grandparents turned back to Jojo, he was sure Aunt Pen grinned and winked. Just a moment. Just a small one.

'We nearly fell to our deaths,' he said.

'Well . . .' said Aunt Pen.

'We were almost crushed in a tunnel.'

'I got you out of there.'

'I was kidnapped by sea creatures.'

'You sort of did that yourself, staring at mermen is never a good idea.'

'Then you abandoned me in that cave!'

'You knew the way out. And here we are. All safe and sound.'

Everyone looked now from Jojo to Aunt Pen. The faerie did not speak. She waited for Jojo. Everyone waited for him. Still he hesitated.

Jojo took another long puff on his asthma pump. 'But . . .' he said. 'I am remembering. And . . .' He trailed off then. He didn't know how to explain the bigger plan at work, the game he thought Aunt Pen was playing. He just could not say what he believed this adventure led to. Now he'd tasted hope, he could not dash it all by speaking its name.

'What?' said Grandad. 'Remembering what?

'I'm remembering . . . him. I'm – I'm remembering Dad.'

Grandad gulped. Ricco frowned up at his brother. Trevor farted.

'That sounds wonderful,' Grandma whispered. 'To remember my boy. That would be the greatest wish come true. He's gone, you see. I've not seen him for such a long time. Gone.'

Jojo knew what she meant. He wasn't just gone-gone. He wasn't just missing in person. Somehow, he was missing in their minds, in their hearts. He was a big empty space. But to remember . . . it was the greatest gift. That's what he'd tasted.

'That's what I'd wish,' said Grandma, who in all this madness was talking more sense than she had done in years. 'I'd wish to live just one memory again. I think I'd want to do it again. Just one special day.'

Grandad squeezed his wife's hand.

Ricco was sat crosslegged on the carpet. 'That sounds brilliant,' he whispered.

Even Trevor understood this was an important moment. His fart came out as a quiet *PPFFTTT!*

Aunt Pen looked at Jojo. She raised her eyebrows. It was up to him. His choice to continue this journey or not. His choice to plunge them back into the unknown.

The will to act, he thought to himself. I must choose. Eventually. I must choose.

Without a word, Jojo nodded.

'Done,' exclaimed Aunt Pen. She wiggled her nose and blinked. The light was a pulse, a brilliant pulse which seemed to come from all of them and burst out across the room.

And then . . .

Nothing.

'Ooooh,' said Grandma. 'Was that it?'

Aunt Pen stuck a finger in her mouth then stuck the same finger in the air, as if feeling the direction of the wind. 'Hmmm,' she said. 'This is a slow brew, I believe. Might need to wait on this one. Tomorrow, I think. We'll see what we see, tomorrow.'

'Lovely,' said Grandma. 'Just lovely.'

Everyone smiled. Grandad squeezed her hand again.

She deserved one day back. Jojo didn't even mind that they'd probably all be in some deadly danger before the day and the wish was done.

No one spoke for a moment. There was a little *put-put-put* of gases from Trevor's bottom.

'Aha,' came a shout from the kitchen. 'Here's the problem.'

Hob Goodfellow came waddling into the kitchen, brandishing a round stone. A round stone with a hole through the middle. A stone which Jojo recognised.

'That's mine,' said Jojo.

'Well then,' said the goblin. 'It seems you broke the washing machine.'

Jojo took back the hagstone. He placed it together with the nine-sided red-gold coin and the white feather in a little leather pouch which had once belonged to his father. He decided to keep the three close by. He was sure they were important, sure they were the key to some future adventure. He'd need them. He just knew it.

That night, waiting for the wish, Jojo dreamed stranger dreams than ever before.

He dreamed of high mountains and deep caves. He dreamed of drowning and falling. He dreamed of howling dogs and huge stone giants. He dreamed of himself in the middle of it, running, jumping, climbing, swimming, flying, fighting. He dreamed of acting in all that darkness. He was not afraid.

And at the end of his path, two figures loomed, a dark figure with even darker eyes, and smouldering, flame-red hair and a man – Jamie Locke, Jojo's dad.

Make Him Dream

Two figures sat and watched a hill. Today it was an empty hill that Penperro and the Sandman, who had finished his rounds early that night, watched. It was marked by a series of ridges that led to a flat top, ridges that spoke of its past. Empty scars on the land that showed what once had stood here.

An empty space that whispered of memories lost.

This hill, that the two Elfaene watched, had once been a castle. And Maiden Castle had once been a great fort. The greatest in all the land.

But this is not why they watched it.

Maiden Castle hill was a memory of an echo of a dream of another world. It echoed from one world to another. Like so many of the great and ancient buildings of the human world, it marked the spot of a greater and more ancient landmark in that other world beyond our own.

'He must come here soon,' said the Sandman. With his eyes, he saw not just the empty hill there in England, but to Dinn Ainnhir, the citadel on the rock in Elfhaeme. 'He must come to the House of the Nine. It is now the only way.'

'I wonder,' said Penperro, the now wizened faerie, her back bent, her eyes weak, 'if it was always the only way. A knight to return to Elfhaeme, a Locke from Dor to enter the house.'

The Sandman looked from the castle to the old faerie beside him. He seemed to see her anew. He cocked his head and frowned. 'You will tell him?' he said.

Penperro nodded.

'Tell him what you can, while you can.'

Penperro nodded again. While she could. She was failing now, fading from both worlds as magic fades, as a spell fails. Soon she would be gone.

The Sandman nodded. 'And then . . . then he will be alone. Soon it will just be him.' The man in black weighed his stardust sack in his hand as he spoke.

Penperro pulled her eyes from the moon and back to the man of dreams. 'Does it need to be though?' Her serious look was gone and her smile returned. 'Can you make *Jamie* Locke dream?'

The Sandman seemed to think for a moment. Then he nodded. 'It can be done, but she will know. And . . . it will be costly,' he said.

'She knows,' said Penperro. 'She knows by now that the boy will come. Maybe she's known all along. She saw him, in the boat, long ago. What she thinks of that, I do not know. She is as broken as magic is. But this, the right dream, might be the extra help Jojo needs.'

The Sandman nodded. 'It may be.' Neither of the old friends spoke of the cost. They both knew what it meant; to go there, to the house in the other world, would cost the Sandman everything.

And then after a pause in which it seemed all the universe waited: 'What would you have Jamie Locke dream?'

'Have him dream of Jojo, of course,' said Penperro, and with that, the faerie was gone. She had so little time.

The Sandman stayed on. He watched, not the hill now, but the castle in that other world. Dreams would come to an end. And all his purpose would be lost. He would turn back to cold hard rock and watch the world from above, never to return to offer dreams of things unseen to sleeping eyes. Unless . . .

Above the castle a storm swirled. Clouds of black and purple. Shots of lightning. There were crashes above and groans of rock below. All was failing.

'I'm coming, Jamie Locke,' he whispered. Then the Sandman stepped out of our world and was gone.

Young Again

Jojo woke with someone sitting on the end of his bed.

'Do you trust me?' said Aunt Pen. The faerie Aunt Pen, tiny and wrinkled with her parcel and bags slung about her – Penperro.

Jojo coughed and then wriggled till he was sitting up in bed.

It was morning. Summer light was just breaking between the curtains. Jojo looked to his bedside clock. *8:06.*

Jojo rubbed his sleepy eyes and yawned. 'I think . . .' he began. 'I think I know what's happening.'

Aunt Pen nodded encouragingly.

Jojo thought, tried to form the words. 'He's coming back. At least . . . the memories are all coming back.'

'Memories,' said Aunt Pen. 'Yes.' She nodded again.

'But there's more . . .' Jojo gulped. 'There's more to be done. And I . . . I . . .'

'You need to trust me,' said Aunt Pen. She had grown so old. In just the few days she'd been with them, she'd grown so old. Her voice croaked. It was small like her. Her eyes were grown weak. She squinted at Jojo through the thick glasses she now wore.

Jojo frowned. 'You said,' he whispered, eyes flicking to

Ricco, asleep on the camp bed, 'there was a plan here. You said . . . I thought . . . I hoped . . .'

'I know what you hope.'

'It just seems . . . everything seems so . . .'

Jojo's mind went back, back to falling through the air, back to the badgers' tunnels collapsing around them, felt the merboys clawing at him.

'. . . dangerous?' finished Aunt Pen. 'But I haven't let you fall yet, have I? I haven't let you down.'

Jojo remembered. Safe in the tower. Carried by piskies. Pulled from the tunnel. Left in the cave with the stone-men coming for him though. Why did she leave him?

'Why did I leave you?' said Aunt Pen. 'That's a good question. Why do you think?'

Jojo thought about this. Diving back down the steps, into the sea, swimming out, out, out.

'Because,' he said, 'I need to act. I need to choose. I need to want to . . . to finish this. Whatever this is.'

Aunt Pen slowly nodded. 'You don't need me; you're strong, Jojo Locke. You can act.' With that, she hopped off the bed and floated towards the door. With each step she grew and grew until she was back to being full-sized-human Aunt Pen. 'The will to act, Jojo Locke. You have it.'

He didn't need her.

'Aunt Pen,' he whispered, as her hand fell on the door handle. She turned to him, with the faintest smile. 'I do trust you,' he said.

'But,' said Aunt Pen, 'rather importantly – you don't *need* me. What you need, perhaps, is a quiet day.'

Jojo sat up straighter. He frowned a deep frown. He gave a deep sigh. Then he nodded. He nodded and sniffed. 'A quiet day sounds good.'

Aunt Pen smiled. 'Before the end, Jojo Locke,' she said from his bedroom door, 'I will tell you a story. The story you've been waiting to hear. When I do, I will have to leave you, for you will know all you need to know. I will have given you all I can. Finally, brave Jojo, you will have to choose.'

Jojo's frown grew deeper. Once more he sighed. And this from the very heart of him. Once more he nodded.

And then, that solemn moment was broken open by a loud shout from the hallway. The voice shouting, Jojo knew well, but somehow it sounded different. It sounded younger.

'Come on, Jojo,' shouted Grandma. 'Up, up, up, the day is here!'

Then, into the room bustled a lady much younger than Grandma. Her hair was brown, just flecked with grey. Her face was smoother, brighter. Her eyes shone.

But . . . it was Grandma.

'Come, Jojo, look. Look!'

She was past Jojo and looking out of the bedroom window, out to the lane, out beyond.

'Jojo,' shouted Ricco now, bounding out of bed and next to Grandma at the window. 'There's a big tent, Jojo!'

Jojo stared at his grandmother, amazed at her brown hair

and yellow dress. She was so young. But . . . it was Grandma. He turned to Aunt Pen to ask if this was her doing, even though he knew it must be. Aunt Pen was gone. No sign of where.

'Come, on,' the lady at the window said – she must have been ten years younger at least. Jojo gulped, then joined them, looking out across the road to the barn and then the field beyond.

And, as Ricco had said, there was a great tent.

They watched as Grandad walked up the lane. He stopped when he saw the tent. His mouth dropped open. Trevor jumped and barked around him. Then Grandad turned back to the house.

'Marnie!' he called, rushing back to the cottage. 'Marnie. You won't believe this!'

They rushed to meet Grandad by the front door.

'You won't believe what day it—' he was beginning to say as he hung up his coat. Then he saw his wife. Again his mouth dropped open, further this time.

Jojo and Ricco did not speak. They looked from Grandad to the younger Grandma and back again. Trevor did not seem to notice. He walked past her, letting out a little stream of gas as he went.

'Mar-Mar-Marnie?' Grandad said. He dropped his hat and pipe, they simply slipped from his grip.

'Hello, darling,' said the younger Grandma.

'Hello,' Grandad replied. 'You look . . .'

'Young?' said Grandma. 'I feel young. At least, I remember feeling young.'

'. . . beautiful,' said Grandad.

The younger Grandma blushed as Ricco and Jojo looked on. 'Thank you, darling,' she said. 'And I do know what day it is.'

'I don't,' said Jojo.

'Are we camping?' said Ricco.

Everyone grinned at Ricco. Even Jojo knew that was no tent for camping. There was some big event to take place in there.

'Come on,' said the younger Grandma. 'Everyone needs to get dressed. Put on your best. What have you brought with you? I'm guessing you don't have suits?'

Grandma's One Day

In fact the boys found they did have suits waiting for them, laid out on their beds. Trousers and jackets, shirts and elasticated pink ties and even a cream waistcoat.

And when they met back in the hallway, they found Grandad did too, with a yellow tie to match Grandma's yellow dress. And Jojo found a memory.

'I've seen this before,' he said. 'I-I remember this.'

Grandma let out a little laugh. 'You have,' she said.

Grandad's brow creased as if he too was remembering, as if memories, hard fighting memories were battling out. 'You were three,' he said.

'And so cute,' said Grandma. 'A naughty, little squidgy three-year-old.'

'Was I there?' said Ricco.

Jojo was remembering.

He'd held Grandad's hand as they crossed the lane.

Now he walked a little behind the other three as they made their way to the tent, Grandad explaining to Ricco that if Jojo had been three then Ricco would not have been born.

Jojo remembered.

They'd come back from the church in Grandad's Jeep. He loved Grandad's Jeep. Mum and Dad had gone ahead in the black shiny car.

Mum all in white, Dad in his suit and pink tie, matching Jojo's own. They were waiting in the tent, waiting for the guests.

They were waiting in the tent.

Jojo looked up, past his brother and Grandad and Grandma. Trevor had trotted ahead and was waiting at the gate to the field. The tent was open, but Jojo could see nothing within, there was veils of sheer pink material hanging in the way. Not yet.

Were they waiting for him? Was his dad waiting for him?

Ricco ran to Trevor and fumbled with the gate.

'It's a tough gate, that one,' said Grandad, and reached out past Ricco to unbolt it.

Jojo's heart was thumping.

Aunt Pen had said she couldn't do it. But . . . maybe . . . maybe . . .

Jojo couldn't help himself, he ran ahead with Ricco. Ran to the tent entrance. There were voices within. They pulled at the long lengths of fabric that hung in the entrance and . . .

There was no one there.

Ricco ran on in but Jojo stood and gulped, trying to calm his heart. Grandad was there now and put a hand on his shoulder.

'Looks exactly the same,' he said.

'I remember it all,' Grandma said, and twirled past them into the marquee.

Jojo did too.

His dad picked him up and swirled him round. He could remember being held by Dad, remember the smell of him but not his face. Mum kissed him. Then he ran off, running round the empty tables. None of the guests had arrived yet. The whole tent was his.

Ricco was doing just the same now, running between tables, bumping against chairs. Trevor was running and barking with him.

Jojo stood with his grandad and watched Ricco run and Grandma spin. 'I don't understand something,' he said.

'Just one thing?' Grandad chuckled.

OK, there was a lot he didn't understand, but he pressed on. 'Why did we actually go there? Into the past. For your wish. But this –' Jojo looked around at the tent and the tables and treasured memories – 'this isn't the actual, real day.'

'Mmm,' said Grandad. 'And why does Marnie get to be young again when I remained an old man?'

Jojo had not thought of this but, 'Yes,' he said.

'I couldn't say, Jojo,' said Grandad. 'But if I had to guess, I'd say that Aunt Pen or whoever else is behind all this, is a darn-sight wiser than you'd credit them. They know not just what we wish for but what we actually need. Look at her!' he finished, his eyes fixed on Grandma, who a day before had struggled to fix her own tea but now laughed and danced, plucking a flower from one of the tables.

Jojo nodded. *What we need.* Not what we want. That truth sunk into his heart like an anchor.

'Look at this,' Ricco called. 'There's a book.'

All three joined Ricco at the long table at the very front of the room. And when they got there, Grandma let out a high-pitched scream of delight.

'Oooohhh! That's my photo album,' she said. 'I thought . . . I thought it was gone. All gone.'

Right at that moment, another scream could be heard: three miles away at the station of Dor, a train pulled to a halt, with a screaming of old brakes. When the train had fully stopped, only one person climbed from the open doors down to the platform – a woman with long braided hair, a smart black business dress and a black leather bag that showed just how prepared for anything she was.

The woman took a deep breath, inhaling the country air in through her nose then out in a long stream through her mouth. She nestled her bag back onto her shoulder and took hold of the small suitcase on wheels that sat behind her.

'Come on then, Lizzie,' she said. 'We're here.'

Lizzie Locke did not like coming to Dor, for the obvious reason that it was the place where her husband had disappeared. But Lizzie Locke kept coming to Dor, for the obvious reason that it was the only connection she had left to the husband who had disappeared. Vanished, not just from the world, but from her heart and her mind.

Lizzie hurried along the platform.

163

Besides, her boys were waiting for her. By some miracle, or magic, or faerie bewitchment, her boss had called her that morning before work and awarded her an extra few days' holiday. No reason given. He didn't seem quite himself but Lizzie was not going to pass up the chance for time with Jojo and Ricco.

So here she was.

At the end of the platform was a small booth with a sign above it that proudly read *Terry's Taxis*.

Lizzie knew this was a lie; there was only one taxi. Terry was the man who sat in the booth, who always seemed to be sitting in the booth, just waiting for Lizzie to arrive.

'Taxi, madam?' Terry called while she was still a long way off.

Lizzie smiled and nodded. 'Of course, good sir,' she called and began the next leg of her journey toward the cottage in the lane.

✳

At that moment, Jojo, Ricco and their grandparents were sitting at the long table, leaning over the big photo album.

'Look, here you are,' said Grandma.

The photo in question showed a short, pudgy child. He had a furry fuzz of black hair and wore a tiny suit with the same shade of pink tie that Jojo was wearing right then.

'Haha! Look at you,' said Ricco.

In the photo Jojo was holding a hand. But the person whose hand was being held was out of shot.

'And that's your dad,' said Grandad.

Memory.

Jojo remembered how it felt, remembered how Dad's big, rough builder's hand felt in his.

'Your first course is served,' said a gruff voice from low down beside the table.

'Ooooh, Mr Goodfellow,' said Grandma as the tiny hobgoblin leaped up on the table with a flourish and presented them all with a miniature plate of jollof rice, coleslaw and plantain.

✳

'So how's good old London?' said Terry, his eyes fixed on the road, his hands fixed on the steering wheel.

Terry, Lizzie knew, had once been a taxi driver in London, but had moved to Dor as a sort of retirement. It was that sort of place, Dor. A sleepy, seaside town. At least, that's how Lizzie thought of it.

'You know,' said Lizzie from the back of the taxi, her luggage on the seat beside her, as they wound along the narrow country lanes. 'It keeps on, keeping on.'

'Busy, then,' said Terry.

The thought of it made Lizzie yawn, a big, wide, lioness sort of yawn.

'I'll take that as a yes,' said Terry. Then he said, 'Oh no,' and the car began to slow.

'What's up?' said Lizzie, peering over Terry's shoulder and through the windscreen. And there she saw the problem. There was a small hill of grain sitting in the middle of the road and beyond it, a tractor and trailer. A farmer stood beside the grain, shaking his head.

'Afternoon, Terry,' called the farmer. 'Bit of a problem 'ere. I'm gonna kill that boy. Didn't bolt the door of the trailer, did he? Gonna have to stop the combine, aren't we? Disaster. Disaster for you too. No way through, I'm afraid.'

Lizzie breathed in deep again, in at the nose, out through the mouth. 'I'll walk,' she said and put a hand purposefully on her luggage.

As Lizzie was stepping from the taxi, Ricco was finishing his miniature plate of food.

'More photos,' he said, and reached out to turn a page of the album. 'Who's this?'

Jojo looked down and breathed in deep. Grandad was silent. Grandma sighed.

'Who is that?' said Ricco. The picture was of Grandad and Grandma dancing. She wore the same dress, the same shoes, the same everything as she wore right then, sitting before them. Grandad wore a brown suit, a suit they'd never seen before. But Ricco's stubby finger was not pointing at his grandparents. He was pointing at a blurred figure in the background. Most of his face was obscured by Grandma's raised arm but you could see he was tall and broad and the edge of a beaming smile shone out of the photo.

Still silence.

Jojo gulped. 'That's Dad,' he said.

'Ahhh,' said Grandma, 'such a wonderful day.'

BANG!

All four Lockes jumped.

The noise had come from outside. Not a scary bang. A magic bang.

'Fireworks,' said Grandad. 'Remember. There were fireworks!'

It wasn't a long walk from the spilled grain to the cottage. But it wasn't a walk for high heels and a business dress. It definitely wasn't a walk for a wheel-along suitcase. But Lizzie Locke was attempting it all the same.

She'd climbed the first stile into the field, hauling her luggage over the fence, and sunk instantly into the soft ground. Her shoes were now stored in her bag and Lizzie was scrambling barefoot between sheep who crowded the path she was on.

'I'm coming, boys,' she said. 'I'm coming.'

And then she saw it. There in the sky above where she was heading, the stars were out.

Lizzie looked up and around. The sky was blue. The clouds – perfect, fluffy puffs – were few and far between. The sun shone down.

But above the cottage, night had begun. And . . . what was that?

Fireworks.

After their surprise at the early nightfall, Jojo, Ricco, Grandad and Grandma had settled down under blankets to watch the fireworks. Hob Goodfellow had served them roast pork baps with spicy apple sauce.

'It's just magical,' said Grandma. 'This is exactly how it was. Do you remember, Joey? Do you remember?'

Jojo remembered it all too.

They were the first fireworks he'd ever seen. He'd watched from his dad's lap. Mum had held his little hand and he'd gasped and whooped and cheered at every sparkle.

It had still taken quarter of an hour from when she'd seen the night sky to when Lizzie arrived, sweaty, muddy and a little chewed by a passing sheep, in the lane by the cottage.

She took a deep breath, looked up at the final rocket explode, pink and gold in the sky, and then headed towards the tent and into the magic.

'Hello,' said a voice from the shadows beside the tent.

Lizzie peered into the gloom as an old lady appeared, wrinkled and worn, hobbling on a pair of walking sticks. 'Aunt Pen. Is that you?'

The old lady stopped in front of the candlelit tent entrance. She slowly nodded. 'You're just in time for dessert,' she said.

Telling Mum

'Where to start . . .' Aunt Pen said, standing in front of a stunned Mum in the wedding tent. Ricco stood on one side of her and Jojo on the other. Mum was sitting at the long table with a slice of chocolate cake in front of her.

She kept looking at the cake, at the candles, at the tent. 'This is . . . this is . . . this is our wedding.'

'Indeed,' said Aunt Pen. 'How to explain . . .'

But Aunt Pen didn't need to think much longer.

'She's a faerie,' said Ricco. 'She's a proper faerie. Show Mum your wrinkly nose thing.'

Aunt Pen looked at Ricco, then at Jojo – he nodded – then she wrinkled her nose and blinked and she was no longer the ancient woman, Aunt Pen, in her skirts and necklaces. She was Penperro the faerie – old and wrinkled still, but tiny. She stood at Mum's knees and looked up into her shocked eyes.

Mum looked down at the faerie dressed as a pirate.

'Cup of tea?' said a croaky voice from Mum's elbow.

Mum screamed and leaped up, away from the hobgoblin, Mr Goodfellow.

Grandad and Grandma were sitting in chairs off to one side and seemed to be nodding off. Trevor lay at their feet.

Ricco, Jojo and Aunt Pen were left to explain to Mum

what on earth had been going on. The hobgoblin was not helping matters.

'What is that?' yelped Mum.

'He's a goblin,' said Jojo quietly. 'And Aunt Pen is a faerie and she has been granting us wishes. And . . . and . . .'

Jojo did not know how to start explaining the other part. The bigger part. The plan he thought they were all part of.

Mum shook her head and then looked at the three of them. Four of them, including Hob Goodfellow, who put down the tea on the table and backed away, looking sheepish.

Mum shook her head again.

'This is . . . It can't be . . . You're . . .'

She didn't finish any sentences.

Aunt Pen wrinkled and blinked and was back as an old auntie. She coughed violently, her frail body rocking back and forth. Mum looked her up and down.

'She is a faerie,' said Ricco.

'This,' said Jojo gesturing at the tent around them, 'was Grandma's wish.'

'Well . . . OK . . .' said Mum. 'What else have you been wishing for?'

Ricco started. 'I wished for my dreams to come true and we went and had a tea party with badgers.'

'Right,' Mum nodded. 'OK. Badgers.'

Jojo blushed. 'I wished that you would stay one more day with us and . . . well . . . that's when you started burping.'

A tiny angry frown flashed across Mum's brow. Then she

grinned. Then she let out a short laugh. 'I . . . I . . .' she scratched her head. 'OK. What about Grandad?' She took a sip of tea.

'Mr Josephus Locke,' Aunt Pen said, 'wished to see his son one more time.'

'What . . . ?' Mum spluttered her tea across the room. '. . . Jamie . . . Is he . . . ? Can I . . . ?'

'We went back in time, Mum. We saw Dad as a little boy.' A frown had spread across Jojo's face. 'We can't . . . It's not . . . You don't exactly get what you want. We can't just wish Dad back. It's not that . . . simple. But . . .' He did not know how to finish that. An idea was forming in his mind but Jojo could not form it on his lips.

He looked at Aunt Pen. She raised an eyebrow and nodded. 'It's not simple,' she repeated. But Jojo heard what else she had said, days before, to Grandad. *Something can be done about what you would ask.*

Something *must* be done.

'Then,' said Mum, cutting across Jojo's thoughts. She had put the tea to her lips but not taken a sip. Now she did, before continuing. 'I want a wish.'

Aunt Pen did a sort of bow as best as her creaking, aged body would allow.

Mum took another gulp. 'I want to know what happened to Jamie. I *wish* to know what happened to Jamie. What happened to my husband?'

Vanishing Dad. This was it. They'd know, even if Jojo had an idea, now they'd know for certain. This was the answer Mum had been waiting for, for long years.

Aunt Pen looked thoughtful. 'This is difficult.'

'Can't we just go back in time again?' Mum said.

Aunt Pen made another face, another thought. 'We could. We could. But it is dangerous. Everything is dangerous now. And . . . I'm not sure that would be best . . . But . . .' went on Aunt Pen, 'I could show you a memory.'

'But there's nothing,' Mum said, choked up now. She forced her words through teary eyes. 'I wasn't there. I have no memories at all. He kissed me goodbye. I went back to sleep and . . . and . . . he was gone. Everything was gone. I . . . I . . . don't remember.'

Aunt Pen's wizened face wrinkled into a frown. 'Not *your* memory,' she said. Then she looked at Jojo, raised an eyebrow. 'Yours,' she said.

What?

WHAT?!?

'Jojo was there.'

'I was there?' Jojo said.

Mum looked at him. Took a breath. Why didn't he know this?

'You were there,' she said slowly as if she was remembering in that moment. 'I . . . I do remember. Dad took you down to the sea. It was . . . it was . . . a normal day. Dad said . . .' She

173

stopped. Frowned. Closed her eyes. 'He said you were going to the beach. Out on the boat. He said I should sleep. He kissed me goodbye and . . .'

'But,' said Jojo, 'I don't remember. I don't remember that.'

'I didn't remember it . . . till . . . till just now . . . I didn't remember anything. But now . . .'

They were silent then. Mum looked at Jojo; a tear broke from the corner of her eye.

'You don't have to just remember,' said Aunt Pen, breaking the silence. 'We can see. If Jojo will allow us.'

All eyes were on him. 'How? I don't . . .' he began but then stopped.

'No. You don't remember,' said Aunt Pen. 'But it is in there. Forgotten in some dark corner of your mind. The memory is there. I can find it. But I will only do it if . . . if you're ready.'

Mum wiped her eyes and looked again at Jojo.

Jojo gazed back, wide-eyed. He needed to know just as Mum did. 'I am,' he said. 'I want to see. I want us to know.'

'Very well,' said Aunt Pen.

With that she wrinkled her nose and blinked and all the world became light.

The Beginning

When the blinding light had cleared, Jojo was no longer in that grand tent in the field beside the cottage in the lane. Instead he was walking along a sandy path. But something was strange. He was somehow shorter.

What? he said. *Where am I?* But no words came from the mouth of the tiny boy who was walking among the dunes. The boy that was Jojo Locke.

This is the memory, said a voice. A voice he knew was Aunt Pen's even though he didn't hear it. There was no sound, apart from waves, wind and wheeling gulls in the sky above.

He didn't hear Aunt Pen, not with his ears. It was more a thought. A thought he knew was Aunt Pen's. And then she spoke again, as a thought. *We're in your head.*

This is Jojo's head? said another thought-voice which Jojo knew was Mum. *This really is unbelievable.*

Indeed, said Aunt Pen, still just a thought. *But all the same, it is true. We're seeing what Jojo saw from inside his own head.*

It was decided that this memory was not for Ricco. Whatever stood on the other side of this walk through the sand dunes, was not for a five-year-old. Grandad and Grandma decided for themselves, they could not bear to see . . . the ending. So Mum and Jojo set out alone, with Aunt Pen, into the coloured insides of Jojo's mind.

I know this path, said Mum. *At least, I did know it. Once. And now . . . I know this path. This is the path in the dunes. Above the beach. This is the day. I . . . I know it. I remember it was so hot.*

As if to confirm this the little boy, Jojo, stopped and looked out at the sea where the sun glinted off the waves. The moon was out too, as it is on some fine, strange magic mornings. He looked out at the arch – broken now as, somehow, Jojo had broken it in the distant past.

'That's the old door of Dor. See it?' said a real voice from behind the boy. 'I was there when it collapsed.'

That's him. That's him, said Mum's thought-voice.

'Come on,' said Dad. 'Keep on going. Nearly there.'

They wandered on, listening to Dad's footsteps on the soft sand and the sound of something large being pulled along behind him. There was no hurry for the little five-year-old Jojo's legs. They all watched as the world jiggled up and down and up and down as he hopped along the sandy path.

'Look, Dad. Seagull,' said Jojo. A little hand shot out to point at the gulls.

The dunes spread out here, made little hills and valleys, sandy nooks and crevices.

'I remember one time, Grandma . . .' Dad began.

'Mmmm,' said the little boy Jojo.

'We were on the beach,' Dad went on. 'I was only little. Bit bigger than you maybe—'

'I'm not little,' interrupted the little boy Jojo, stopping on the path again.

Dad gave a little chuckle. 'No, you're not little. I was little though. I put my sandwich down on my towel on the beach and Grandma gave me this big talk about not putting it down cos the greedy seagulls would snatch it and while she was saying this, she'd put her own sandwich down and this seagull came up behind her and snatched it. I laughed and laughed.'

'That's so funny,' said the little Jojo.

That's brilliant, said Jojo's thought-voice. *Only Grandma.*

I remember that story. Now . . . I remember . . . Mum's thought-voice said. *How did I forget? Why did I forget?*

That is the question that must be answered, said Aunt Pen.

They went just a little further along the path, before they came to the top of a ridge: 'Right. Here we are.' They heard his voice above Jojo's head as he looked out at the wide beach below them. 'Climb in,' said Dad, 'I'll pull you right down to the waves now.'

Jojo turned then to his dad, dressed in red shorts and a T-shirt with tiny pictures of sailing boats on it, as Dad leaned down towards him.

That's the shirt. That's the shirt he wore, said Mum's thought-voice. *I remember. I remember it now. I didn't but . . but now . . . I remember.*

'Come on,' said Dad. He crouched and lifted five-year-old Jojo, swinging him round and placing him in the red boat he was dragging along behind him on the same two-wheeled trailer they'd seen in Grandad's past.

Jojo stamped his little feet on the wooden boards inside.

'Comfy?' said Dad.

The picture went up and down as Jojo nodded. Then they were off, trundling down the dune path towards the flat sand and gentle, rolling sea beyond.

Dad sang as they made their way across the beach.

I would take you there, to the land beyond the sea,
I would take you there and all that we would be,
Are unremembered echoes, passing through the mind,
Unless they too pass through the arch: those we left behind.

I know this song, said Jojo by thought and feeling. He did know it. He knew it deep within. They knew it in their bones. Grandma had sung it to them. It coursed through them as a raging river of memory as the boy in the boat and his singing father made their way down towards the waiting waves.

I would take you there, beyond the arch of stone,
To the endless rolling hills the hidden folk call their home,
To the faes' unfading woods, alive with magic strong,
To the mountains capped with ice, to caverns filled with song.

I would take you there, to the land of the elven kind,
From the imp, the hob, the sprite, to the faerie sisters nine,
Those hidden, mystery folk, faces bright with shining eyes,
Whose long lives flit between their world and the
    land of you and I.

I would take you there, to see the storied shining stars,
I would take you there, but we must not journey far,
We must not tarry long, or for ever we will dream,
Of wood and hill, mount and moon that ever gleams.

Unless they too pass the arch, left behind we'd be,
As unremembered whispers, in the land beyond the sea.
I would take you there and there we'd stay unless,
The song is sung and all put right, unless my son, unless . . .

They arrived beside the sea and Jojo knew then what had happened. It was there in his mind to be brought forth and inspected as clear as the seabed that the young Jojo leaned over the boat's edge and surveyed with wide-eyed curiosity.

The picture rocked and a clunk and rattle told them that Dad was busy unloading the boat into the ankle-deep water. Jojo kept his gaze fixed on the seabed.

'Fish,' said the little boy. 'Fish, Daddy.'

The Lockes saw through the child's eyes the cream and brown speckled fish, almost camouflaged, half buried in the sand. Its big pupils stood out black. It blinked and at the same moment a yell sounded. A roar.

What's happening? Mum whispered as the vision flew around, searched from boat to sky to sea. No Dad.

The little boy Jojo scampered across the boards to the back of the boat. Then they saw him. Dad lay in the wash of the shallow sea. He clutched his right foot. His face was scrunched, folded inward, his teeth bared, his breaths coming in ragged choking hacks.

The picture filled with tears. 'Dad, Dad, Dad,' the little Jojo gasped.

What is wrong? What happened? Mum's thought-voice whispered again.

'Daddy,' said little Jojo as tears flooded the vision and desperate sobs shook it.

No. No. No, Mum whispered.

'Jojo,' Dad looked up at his son. Straight into his eyes. 'You need to go . . .' he winced, '. . . and get help. Weever fish . . . tell them, weever fish.'

Weever fish, Mum said. *What's . . . what's that? What does he mean?*

Aunt Pen had not thought aloud for some time but broke her silence now. *It's a very nasty little fish. Just like the one Jojo saw. It waits in the sand and uses its poisonous barbed back as a defence. I'm so sorry.'* She linked her hand through Mum's.

The little boy's eyes closed as fresh tears sprung with his strangled sobs.

'Jojo!' Dad was as loud as he could manage. 'Look at me . . . weever fish . . . Say it.'

His breathing was now like sandpaper over metal.

'Weever fish . . . say it.'

'We . . . we . . . weever fish,' Jojo cried.

Dad still did not move from where he lay amongst the

waves. His face creased into a wince every few seconds. 'Climb down . . . onto me,' he said. 'Don't . . . tread . . . on this . . . sand.'

Jojo did as he was told, clambering from the red boat onto his father's chest. He lay then, face to face, tears from the child's eyes falling onto the man's dark cheeks and running off into the sea which swirled around them.

'Be brave, little one,' Dad whispered, squeezing Jojo tight. 'Run now . . . get help.'

Jojo was gulping at the air and nodding. 'I'll run so fast, Daddy,' he said.

'I . . . know you will . . . buddy.' Dad's face disappeared into another agonised wince and then, 'Ready?'

Little Jojo nodded. Dad squeezed him tight and then breathed twelve final words, 'Don't worry, little man . . . Don't look back. It's going to be . . . OK.'

And that was it. Jojo knew now. The final words he heard his dad speak and the first that he remembered. The first memory to break free. The words that had set this chain in motion.

Then five-year-old Jojo was up and running. He did run fast. Behind him there was a noise like a rushing wind. It was altogether extraordinary on that clear day. But Jojo did as his dad requested. He didn't look back. He looked up.

And there, appearing as if by magic, was a tiny figure no bigger than the boy himself. She wore brown leather boots, striped black and red trousers, a burgundy gold-buttoned jacket and a pirate hat. She was not old and white-haired. But it was, most definitely . . . Aunt Pen.

You, said two thought-voices together.

Me, said the thought-voice of Aunt Pen. *I came as the world broke, as that which must be remembered was forgotten.*

In the vision Aunt Pen looked past the boy, out to sea, towards the stone arch. Her eyes were locked. Her brow was furrowed. She wrinkled her nose and blinked. Then all went white. All was light again.

Back in the field across the lane from the cottage, which they'd never really left, the Lockes were catching their breath. Jojo reached for his asthma pump, pulling it past the pouch which held the feather, the holed-stone and the coin – he kept these always with him now.

The tent had gone, tables and chairs and candles too. The wedding was all wrapped up and they stood simply in the grassy field on a summer's day. Jojo was no longer in a suit but in a plain hoody, jeans and trainers.

'What . . . what happened?' Mum was crying and forced the words out between chattering teeth. 'Did you help him?'

But neither of these questions were answered.

The faerie – slight, wizened and frail – stumbled forward. She looked up into Jojo's eyes. She opened her mouth as if to speak but then . . . she was gone.

There was no puff of smoke, no flash of light, no magic

to mark the passing of Penperro, Third Queen of Elfhaeme. All that was left was a yellowing envelope which drifted down through the air so slowly, it was as if it was itself unable to believe she was gone.

Jojo reached out and plucked it from the air.

Let me tell you a story, it read on the front of the envelope.

'This is it,' said Jojo. He knew it was the end of the story. Then he sat there amongst the wildflowers and read the story that his faerie godmother could not speak when she was still with him.

Let Me Tell You a Story

There were once nine sisters. Nine faeries. Nine queens. You can read about them all through history, myth, legend. You can read about us. Nine witches, we've been called. Nine sorceresses. Nine muses.

Once there were three, as old as song, as old as the very first action, as old as memory.

Then there were six – the second of three to be the beginnings and the strife and the end.

Last there were nine – the final three to govern sky and land and sea.

This story is not just of those sisters though.

There was once a family. They've been a famous family. They've been a lost family. They are an old family. They've been called the royal Pendragons, the lowly Lincolns, the Loswells, the fierce Rowlands, the De Frobervilles, the Griffiths, the Troughtons and now the brave house of Locke. The name has changed but the family line remained.

These two families, the sisters nine and the Lockes, have become, through time and chance, adventure and misadventure, entwined. Your story and our story are the stories we're here to tell. But not all. All would take time as there is so much that I could tell.

I could tell you the tale of my sister, Morgana, queen of the land, and the great king, Arthur Pendragon. Or the story of his son Tom, a Lincoln, and his marriage to my sister Caelia Ceridwen, who is called Melete, who must act, for that is what she does, who she is. We could spend long evenings recounting the tales of the first to take the name, the Faerie Knight and her brother, the Black Knight, and their journeys through our worlds. I could whisper of my sister Nymphidia, queen of all beginnings, and her troubles with Pigwiggen Loswell – I know, I know an altogether silly name – but another to take the title Faerie Knight. I could speak of the bloody tale of Childe Rowland and how he came to Elfhaeme seeking my sister Morrigan who is called Moronoe, who had taken as her maid his sister, Ellen. We could talk on the life of Marnie de Froberville and her travels with the explorer, my sister, Polperra, maiden of the sea. I could tell all about young Elsie Griffiths and her troubles with piskies and the help that came from the land of faerie in the shape of the first of us, my sister Aoede, the singer of the song.

But time we do not have for every tale I could tell. We have time for scattered pieces of but one story. The story is of Jamie Locke and my sister, the faerie of endings, the faerie of death – Mabivissey.

Jamie Locke, son of Marnie Troughton, was young when he first met my sister. He was seven. She was . . . well . . . a few millennia older, shall we say. But she was taking a turn in the other world, your world. Living a life as a simple farm girl in the village of Dor.

Sometimes, we will do such a thing, it allows us to see further, see deeper, reminds us of who we are, reminds us of the sacred things we guard – memory, actions, endings.

When Mab set forth, she was warned, as we all are.

In fact it was I, as the only one of the three not now sleeping, who gave her these warnings:

Don't use magic where the eyes of mortal men pry.

Don't play the kinds of tricks our sort have become known for.

But above all, do not fall in love —tragedy has only ever come from the love between a faerie and a human.

So what did she do? She used magic. She would show the other children of Dor marvels. She'd whisper down buzzards from the sky, call up fish from the stream, enchant all manner of creature of the fields and have them play around her. She'd appear in places she had no business being. And for a while Jamie Locke was entranced by these wonders.

She played tricks. They'd play hide and seek in the woods. But my sister would not play fair, hiding within a dandelion head or a mouse's nest. She'd hide items too, items which belonged to Jamie, she'd hide them in impossible places before returning them. He thought her marvellous fun.

They grew up together, here in Dor.

And, she fell in love.

How do I know all of this?

Because I watched. It was my job, my promise, to watch over seven generations of de Frobervilles and Troughtons and now Lockes. To be their faerie godmother.

It was my job and I failed.

She will forget him, I thought. She will come back home when her seventeen years end. She will come home and continue as Mabivissey, continue to bring endings at their proper time, to close and cut off, to unwind and wrap up, to stopper and shut.

But she did something I knew nothing of, which she went to great lengths to deceive me of. She set a plan to hold back death — the one thing she is charged with welcoming.

She took from your father a token he did not know he carried. A singular token, the coin that all humans carry, secret even to themselves, each one unique, each written with a name and an hour – the hour that death must come.

She hid that coin away. But at just the right time, she appeared, not to bring death but to force life.

She stole him away to a place you have seen, to that other world, my world, to a castle, Dinn Ainnhir, the House of the Nine.

I have not been able to speak to her since that day. None have. The place where she keeps him is well guarded by magics only the unraveller can unravel. And she will not.

And I imagine she believed that this would be the end of it. He was taken. Her deed was complete. But that act was not an ending but a beginning – the beginning of the ending.

The queen of death had fallen. She had broken her vow and so broke our world open. She broke apart the very fabric of all the magical contracts between the two worlds. And now, all magic, all power, all light and life is sinking away into the cracks she's made.

And soon, like me, it will come to an end.

Unless . . .

As the end approaches, even the dark magics my sister wove begin to weaken. And one faerie, who had failed above all others, the guardian of remembrance, was able to wake memories across the worlds.

And now there is one in Elfhaeme who remembers, who is trying to come home.

As the end approaches, another guardian, one of dreams, saw what could be done. So together, dream and memory came to you. Managed to smuggle you, for just a moment, to that place. Gifted you what we could – memory and dream.

And here you are, the only one with the keys to free Jamie Locke. One with a magic more powerful. One who could change everything.

And here are my final gifts:

Courage, take hold of it.

The will to act, let it take hold of you.

Fire, deep inside, you will need it at the end.

It is up to you, Jojo Locke.

This is the final testimony of Mneme Thalia Penperro, guardian of memory, queen of Elfhaeme, the Third of Nine.

The Will to Act

The final words of Aunt Pen cast her final spell. A flash of light and Jojo Locke was alone in the field as thunder cracked and lightning flashed and one by one, huge drops of rain began to fall.

It is up to you, Jojo Locke, she'd written. Jojo played back other words, things said by his faerie godmother over the past few days. Memories he watched again. He tried to piece together wishes that had unravelled as he got wetter and the night got darker.

It was all a puzzle.

Something can be done about what you would ask. Those words seemed to come from long ago.

If his dad was where she said he was . . . If it was all real and true and he had to believe it was . . . What could he do? How could he even get there without . . .

Then a thought came to him, it dropped into his brain like a boulder – solid and certain.

Faerie mounds!

Jojo clicked on his phone. He huddled over it to shield it from the rain. He needed to know something and somehow, magically, his phone was working. He had full signal. He went online and typed in two words:

Thrice widdershins

Widdershins is a term meaning to go anticlockwise, one website told him.

And another, *From Middle English, thrice means repeated three times.*

'OK, OK,' said Jojo aloud to no one. 'In a thunderstorm. So . . .'

With that he took a deep breath and pulled up his hood. Out of the darkness a yapping, farting dog came running.

'Good boy,' said Jojo. 'You know, don't you? I can't do this alone.'

✳

Once they walked the long trek into the village and into the park, it did not take Jojo and Trevor long to find the stony path to the faerie mounds. It did not take them long to be soaked to the skin either.

'This way,' Jojo said to Trevor.

Jojo did not try to send Trevor back. He was glad of the company. Even if it was just a dog. It kept his heart from leaping up into his throat every time the thunder struck. It stopped his teeth from chattering from the cold. It forced him to take each step forward.

'Come on, Trevor.'

On they went along the path, shivering. Every so often Trevor stopped and shook himself, sending water spraying in all directions. It did not make Jojo wet though. He was already as wet as one could be.

They pressed on through the driving rain, keeping the loose stone of the path at their feet.

They almost missed the faerie mounds. If the storm had not thrown lightning across the sky at that precise moment then they would have walked on by. Instead they stopped and Jojo stared into the pitch-black night to the left of their path.

'Was that . . . ? Did you see it, Trevor?'

Trevor did two things at once. He barked and he farted. Did this mean yes?

Jojo ignored the dog and continued to stare. There! The lightning struck again, light rebounding off a million raindrops. The low mounds sprung up before them.

'OK,' Jojo said. 'Widdershins. Anticlockwise. That means we go . . . right. This way, Trevor.' With that he set off into the dark again, cutting a path to the right of the faerie mounds. He continued on, curving slightly to the left until he felt the ground rise a little: the edge of one of the miniature hills. He needed to go round them.

'Nope,' he said. 'A bit further.'

A bit further they went, boy and dog, cutting a path through the storm, round the faerie mounds, untangling themselves from bramble bushes, pulling a trainered foot from boggy mud. Each time the lightning struck, Jojo wiped the rain from his eyes and, sighting the mounds on their left, he realigned their course and set off again until they found themselves back on the stones of the path.

'That's once,' said Jojo. He did not stop but set off again.

This time the path was easier. They could almost see where they'd stepped before. They avoided the brambles. Only sank a little into the bog. And found themselves back again on the path.

'Twice.'

Trevor barked at this news.

Once more they stepped off the path, round the brambles, through the bog, through the driving rain.

Lightning struck as Jojo stopped. The path was but a few steps away. All he saw was the mounds to their left and the pebble path before them. But he knew, he felt it as a trickle of electricity down his spine, that far more lay ahead.

'This is it,' he whispered to the dog. 'Don't get scared now.' These last words he said to himself. He took a deep breath. Took his asthma pump from his hoody pocket. Took a puff, thought of his dad and stepped on.

A foot on the path and like magic, the rain stopped. The lightning stopped. No longer was it dark. But it was not day either.

Elfhaeme

Jojo looked around in the dim, dusk light, under that purple and black sky that he'd seen over this land on the first day he'd met Aunt Pen. This was the place. He knew it. He knew it deep in his bones. He was no longer in his own world. He was in that other place.

'We're here, then,' said Jojo quietly. 'The Land of Faerie. It's not nice, is it?'

To his right all was desolate, quiet wasteland.

To his left, where the faerie mounds had been, was something like a village. The houses were tall, and pointed, like cylindrical cans with witches' hats propped on top. They were dotted with circular windows. None showed light or any other sign of life. The cobbled paths that ran between them were choked with weeds.

'Hello?' Jojo called. 'Hello!'

No answer; the village was long abandoned.

In front of Jojo, where Trevor now shook the rain from his coat, was the sight which really drew the eyes though.

The ground was split. We are not speaking here of a slight crack. Not a gully. It was a vast canyon. The edge, ten metres away, was too close for Jojo's liking. And he did not need to venture closer to see just how deep the chasm was. It stretched out before them, deep and wide. It was an abyss, dwindling away into darkness.

Where was the water? Jojo thought. Last time he'd been here, that chasm had held a stormy sea. Now it was nothing but nothingness.

Trevor barked, his nose pointing ahead.

Jojo followed his gaze. There, far out in the middle of the empty nothingness of the gulf was an island. And on it a tiny speck of a castle. *The* castle.

And once again, Jojo was struck by a certainty, deep inside. That was where his father was.

'I see it,' said Jojo. 'But how can we . . . ?'

Courage.

Jojo took a step forward. Trevor farted loudly. 'Come on,' the boy said.

Another step. Trevor farted again but this time followed. Closer and closer they came to the edge. Each step an effort of will.

The will to act.

Jojo swallowed. Even as the rain chilled him, a sweat broke out on his forehead. He squeezed his hands tight together as he reached the edge of the huge ravine.

'Well,' he said, turning back to Trevor, who had stopped several paces back. 'What now?' Were they to step out into the dark? Step into nothing?

Trevor barked.

The only one with the keys . . .

The thought came to him on the wind, carried from his own world.

Keys. Jojo reached into his jeans pocket, expecting to find the feather and the pouch. Instead, he was struck by a strange tingling across the back of his hand. He quickly pulled it back and then screamed at what he saw.

His hand, which he was certain had gone into his pocket quite ordinary, had come out covered in feathers. Not a random scattering of feathers. These were arranged and preened as on a great bird's wing.

Feathers?

Jojo recovered himself, remembering the wings from just a few days before, and reached in once more. The same tingle, the same feeling, but he groped with feathered fingers and pulled out the feather.

It was white and gold as he remembered. But now it glowed, somehow whiter than white. It burned bright. Jojo had to turn his eyes to one side.

He took a deep breath, passed it from his left hand to his right and watched as the back of this hand sprouted feathers too.

Jojo looked at his plumed hands, looked at the feather.

He pulled off his sodden hoody, making sure to retrieve the asthma pump and push it into the empty pocket of his jeans.

This would work. This had to work.

He held the feather by the shaft and slowly ran it from his

left hand across his wrist, forearm, elbow. The same frisson of electricity. The buzzing tingle. Feathers, white and speckled with brown, sprang from his skin, sprouted and grew.

And grew.

And it was not just the feathers that grew. Jojo felt a shiver run the length of his arm. It juddered and shook and then with a jolt of pain his bones began to lengthen.

He let out a short cry. Trevor barked in reply.

But Jojo did not stop – the will to act. He continued with the feather, playing across his upper arm to his wet T-shirt and shoulder.

And still it grew. And grew and grew. Till it was no longer an arm. His limb was now vast and feathered. Jojo stretched out the fully formed wing. It was huge. Two metres, perhaps. Maybe more.

He'd not really looked at the wings the last time. It had all happened so quickly.

Somewhere in there was a hand. Jojo tried wiggling his fingers. There was a ruffling in the furthest feathers. Hmmmm . . . no hand?

Jojo looked from the feather in his right hand to the wing stretched out to his left. He tried pulling it in. It tucked into place if he pulled where his left hand should have been up toward his face.

Trevor barked.

'I know, boy. I know,' said Jojo. 'Pretty freaky.'

Jojo looked back at Trevor.

If the dog was going to come with him . . .

'OK, boy.'

Trevor yapped as Jojo approached.

'Sit still.'

He sat still, letting out the smallest of whispered farts.

'Let's try this . . .'

Jojo did not run the feather down Trevor's forelegs. Instead, he tickled it across Trevor's back.

The dog yapped and wriggled.

'Shhh . . . shhh . . . shhh,' Jojo said and held him still under his feathered left arm.

Where the feather touched him, more feathers spread and grew, as on Jojo's arm. They were brown and careworn, like Trevor's fur. They seemed somehow to fit him.

Trevor yelped again and shifted under Jojo's arm. From somewhere bones sprung from his back taking the feathers up with them. Jojo went on till Trevor had a full pair of wings protruding from his right shoulder blades.

Jojo stood and looked at the now-winged dog.

'Well,' he said, 'that worked.'

Trevor barked and barked and did not now sit. He did not wait. He stretched the wings. He took a step, took a run and then leaped forward, beating his new limbs. Each little fart propelled him forward as Trevor's paws left the ground, as he flew.

'Hold on, Trevor,' called Jojo, as the dog barked and glided above him. 'Don't go far.' Trevor barked again in reply.

Jojo placed the spiny end of the feather carefully into his mouth. He ran the feather down his right arm – the same sprouting feathers, the same lengthening bones, the same tingling pain – till he too had a pair of wings.

As the feather reached his shoulder blade, the glow that had bathed everywhere it touched died. The feather withered in his mouth. It shrank and crumbled and then blew away as dust.

'I guess that's all we get then,' Jojo said, frowning. He had half a thought that he would use the feather to remove the wings, in reverse somehow. That hope was gone.

Well, he thought, winged was better than gilled. At least he got to fly.

To fly . . .

Trevor now was flapping and barking like he'd been born to fly, like he'd always known how. And Jojo knew why. The white feather had brought not just wings but knowledge too.

Jojo stretched his own wings. He did not need to think what to do next. He stepped and beat and ran and beat again. He gasped as he rose over the canyon.

Jojo joined Trevor the barking, farting, flying dog.

'Woooof!' said Trevor.

Jojo did not wait to weigh up their next move. He acted. With a beat of his huge wings he set out for the House of the Nine.

Across the Abyss

Jojo tried not to look down, for when he did, the dark of the chasm seemed to swallow him. It was all he could do to drag his eyes away before he began to plummet, before he gave himself into the arms of that darkness.

'Don't look down, Trevor! Don't look down.'

There was no fear of that. Trevor was paying little attention to the great opening below them. He had his little doggy eyes fixed firmly on the castle up ahead. With his tongue lolling out of his mouth to one side, wispy farts escaping in the breeze, Trevor was flapping forward as happily as he would have been running through the woods beside Grandad. His tail wagged and wagged.

'Good dog,' said Jojo, steering his own eyes to the castle, the house at the centre of all this. 'Good dog.'

The castle. It grew now. It was a grey tooth erupting from a rocky gum. Grey and sheer, it went up and down, with no cavities, no gaps, no doors, no gates, no caverns, no ways in or out. It erupted with a cacophony of towers, each topped with a pointed fairytale black roof.

The purple and black clouds did not streak above these but circled them like halos of doom.

'That's where we're going,' Jojo said, swooping in beside

Trevor, pushing down the question of how they would get in. Surely a door would present itself.

The dog barked and wagged his tail.

As the towering island of rock grew, so did Jojo's certainty. This was their destination. This was where each moment of magic had been heading.

Jojo looked back for a moment to the abandoned village, which in his world had been simple mounds. It was grown small now. Minute. It was a collection of specks on the distant cliff.

His eyes swivelled back to the castle. Jojo began to see the scale of the great place. It was as tall as the tallest buildings in London. Taller. The cloud-wreathed tops seemed to stretch like fingers, reaching upwards even as he watched.

'Nearly there,' he whispered.

And as he did, he saw them. Jojo and Trevor were not the only figures flying in that strange sky.

He'd missed them before. Perhaps they'd been hidden behind the towers. Perhaps they'd been further away, just now swooping in towards the castle. But there they were. A boy and a girl. A boy with dark skin and a girl with red hair.

There was no doubting who they were.

They glided together, spiralled and plunged downward. They were birds, flying for the sake of flying.

They were angels, figures from the other side of death.

Was this it? Did he merely need to fly on, to reach out a hand and take his father back?

He could not stop himself; he opened his mouth and called out, 'Dad! DAD!'

His boy-father turned. They were close enough that Jojo could read that young face. Surprise first, then recognition. His father opened his mouth. He reached out his own hand as if to wave. And then he was gone. Vanished.

The same could not be said for the girl. Her face darkened. Her brow creased. She screamed. A wordless, raging scream.

Jojo did not answer but the clouds did. They did not crackle and thunder as the clouds in Dor. They made no sound, neither did they break into rain. They simply began to descend. And descend quickly.

So quickly that the tops of the towers and the flying girl were hidden in moments. Seconds, and the castle was halved in height.

The darkness welled below and the clouds fell from above.

'OK,' said Jojo. 'OK.' Knowing now that this rescue mission, as that is what it surely was, would not be as simple as a wave of a magic feather.

What to do? What to do? Jojo had moments to make a decision. Let the clouds take them. Or descend into the abyss.

Trevor farted and barked as one.

Jojo took a breath and steeled himself. 'Courage!' he shouted, setting his face at the sky. 'Come on, dog,' he said and took the fight to the clouds, beating his wings, and with each push, propelling himself upward and forward.

Jojo had once walked in mist, on an early morning trot with Grandad. He expected the clouds to be much like that. He expected them to hit him with a wave of cool dampness.

He was wrong.

The waves came down and bathed them in warmth. Jojo and Trevor did not shiver with cold but jangled as if a small jolt of electricity ran through them.

Around them all was swirling purple and black, dark with shadows, lit here and there with breaking shafts of yellow light from above.

Jojo gulped, looked to his left, to his right.

Trevor? Where was Trevor?

'Trevor?' he called. But the clouds acted like a thick duvet. His voice escaped his mouth and then fell, sucked in by the dark pillows.

'Trevor?' he tried again, louder now as another shot of electricity ran through him. The feeling was familiar. It was much like the feeling of the feather, running over his arms. But this was fainter.

'TREVOR?!' Jojo tried once more, louder still, his body shaking with the effort. His body shook and feathers scattered from his wings, floating away out of sight.

Somewhere far away the dog barked.

Trevor barked again and another shot of electricity rocked through Jojo's body. Feathers scattered again.

'No . . . no . . . no!' Jojo looked to his wings. They were sparser somehow. Still there. Still beating him forward. But with each flap, feathers fell. A gap. He saw a gap. His heart leaped into his mouth. She'd not sent the clouds to blind them, but to kill them.

How close to the castle had they been? If the wings failed now, could they make it? How far would they fall?

'TREVOR!' he called again. But what could the dog do? His wings would fail just as surely as Jojo's would.

'No!' Jojo whispered. 'NO!' he shouted at the clouds.

Another wave of electrical magic shot through him. He saw this one, it beat a glowing blue from his chest out to the tips of his wings.

Feathers came away in chunks now. And he was falling. Not straight down. Falling with each beat of his ragged wings to who-knew-what landing.

'Aunt Pen,' he whispered. 'Aunt Pen, if you have anything, any way to help, now's the time.'

He heard Trevor's distant bark as if he too was calling for help.

He beat his wings once more. They were still more wing than not, but only just. Only just, and they had grown smaller.

But as he flapped, a flash of light cut through the clouds. And in that moment, he saw Trevor. He saw Trevor and he saw a rocky cliff face with a narrow, jagged crevice cut into it. An opening with a waterfall pouring forth. It was close.

'This way, Trevor,' Jojo cried.

The dog saw him, barked and wriggled, wagging and flapping toward him.

'We can make it!'

The clouds closed again and electric magic rang through him again. Feathers now fell like rain.

He no longer had wings. He had arms. Arms, which flapped uselessly.

He heard Trevor beside him. Jojo reached out and caught him, clutched onto his hairy form. They tumbled together, still hurtling forward.

Jojo screamed. Trevor barked.

Then all went dark.

All went wet.

A Forest in the Deep

Jojo and Trevor had landed, not splat on the side of a cliff, but into the river at the base of the cave they had made for. They crashed into the water which slowed them just enough that as they hit the craggy bottom, they did not break. Momentum threw them forward through the dark current. Jojo's arm and back crunched along the rocks beneath him.

Soaked again, bruised and shaking, they bobbed to the surface as the water began to pull them back the way they'd come, toward the waterfall at the entrance.

The river sped toward this drop, dragging them onward. They had not fallen into the abyss, but if they did not escape the river, they soon would.

Jojo clung on to Trevor. The dog yelped and struggled, kicking against Jojo. Jojo would not let him go.

The boy kicked forward and reached with his free hand. He pulled them both from the water, dropping a sopping wet dog on the stone bank.

Trevor stood and shook while Jojo lay, shivering.

Jojo lay a long time. His feet were still in the river. His body was splayed across the rock of the cavern floor. Trevor sat by his side, farting every so often.

Had they failed, Jojo thought. Was this it? The end, in a cave below the castle. One sight of Dad. That was all he got.

The gushing of the water echoed through the chamber.

A river. A river must come from somewhere.

Slowly, feeling each bruise along his back, Jojo rose. He shook himself, a last few soggy feathers falling to the floor.

The river did lead somewhere. Away from the crack in the cliff, the water led to another opening, a dark, dark hole. There was enough bank for Jojo and Trevor to pass beside the river. The opening was just tall enough for Jojo.

Courage.

'We'll go on, boy,' Jojo said, and strode on towards the blackness deep within the cave. He dropped to his knees and they crawled into the opening.

Jojo felt his way ahead with hands on the rough stone. He could hear the water to his left and Trevor panting behind him. There was no light apart from the glimmer of the opening at the mouth of the cave which faded with each shuffle forward.

'I don't know where this goes, Trevor,' Jojo said. A sharp pain ran up his knee as he ground it onto a jagged stone.

It could go nowhere, he thought.

Hope diminished as quickly as the light did.

But what choice did they have? There was no way back. No way to get out of that cave. Unless they could scale the cliff? Impossible.

Jojo continued on, into the dark. The chief fact that kept him going was that the tunnel did slope upwards – that, at least, was the way they wanted to be going. Up toward the castle.

The sound of rushing water. The warm panting of the dog. The feeling of the rough stone beneath him was all he had to go on. But something changed in those sounds and feelings, something that told him there was a little more room. They were in a wider tunnel now – maybe the ground was even smoother, maybe these stones had not just formed here. Maybe they'd been placed here?

Jojo reached up with his right hand, steadied himself with his left. There was space above him. He went from his knees to a crouch. Still some space. Then, slowly, he stood. His hand found the ceiling now, at least a foot above him. He looked up and saw it, a dark shape on a dark ceiling.

'That's better,' he said to Trevor. 'Now, if only—'

He had been going to say, *If only there was some light*. But before he could, he realised there *was* some light. There must be. If he could see his hand.

He brought it towards him. He could definitely see it. His hand.

'Trevor, Trevor,' Jojo hissed. 'Do you see that? Light.'

The dog barked. Jojo heard his tail swishing along the floor.

Light.

'Come on.'

On they went. Without his hands on the floor, they went

quicker. But Jojo found when his foot caught on a protruding rock that speed was not everything. He tumbled forward, putting out hands and holding his breath. Where would he land?

He hit the ground, slipped and held on. He had no way of knowing how deep or how strong the river was in this part of the cave. But he could hear it. It sounded further away, as if at the bottom of a steep bank.

Trevor barked and leaped at him, clinging on to his ankles. But he didn't slide away.

'Phew. That was close,' Jojo muttered. 'Good boy.'

He saw the dog now. Trevor's gentle brown face was pushed towards his. The dog licked him. On a normal day Jojo wouldn't have gone near Trevor's slobbering mouth, but there in the dark cave, lying on the cold floor, it was somehow comforting.

'I'm OK,' Jojo said and stood, resting a hand on the good dog's head.

The light, Jojo could see now, was somewhere ahead. The tunnel they were in was indeed wider. It was almost a hall and at the end it opened out again into some place even grander.

The boy and the dog walked on. How long had they walked? How far? Was it night or day? Did this place even have night and day or was it always that dusk of purple and black?

The end of the tunnel grew brighter. Jojo could now see

the river, ten metres down. It rushed on. They could see the walls and ceiling and floor of the rocky corridor.

'We've nearly made it, Trevor,' Jojo said.

But where had they nearly made it to?

The light ahead was not the warm shining of the sun. It was not the steady glow of electric lights. It was something else. It was golden and orange and seemed to pulse now and then, grow brighter, dimmer. What sort of place was this? Could it be lava? A volcano?

The river now leaped in short waterfalls, coming to the level of the path as they approached the end of the tunnel. Beyond, in the wide, open space, Jojo could see some tall pillars or spires of rock, and the gurgling gush of the river seemed to stop.

When he stepped out of the tunnel into the blue-green wash of light, Jojo could see why. The river was not gone, instead it became a dozen trickling streams, which split and twisted and split again until the floor of that great cavern was running with hundreds of fingers of water. But the pillars these fingers wound around were not pillars at all.

They were trees.

Huge, vast, colossal. As wide as a bus is long, they reached up and up to the roof of the great cavern. Jojo stood and stared. He could not believe the size of the place. How could it even fit within the rock which held the castle? (Come to think of it, how had that never-ending passage fit too?) There must have been hundreds of the trees. Thousands.

They were crowned with the red leaves of autumn. The leaves fell and coated the floor. And it was from these that the strange light came. It would have been bright, up there amongst the treetops, Jojo thought. Below, the falling leaves lost their light as they dropped, till they were like the flame of a match on the floor, guttering out quickly till they burned no more.

Trevor was off, snuffling and scurrying through the leaves, splashing through the nearest streams.

Jojo took a step and caught a glowing leaf as it fell.

He looked at the light. He saw it was not the whole leaf which shone. There was an intricate pattern within the veins, like magic pulsed within those select channels. Jojo held it up, inspected it closer. It was not just a pattern. There was a picture in the light. A portrait.

There, in the lit veins of the leaf was a young woman. The faerie queen. Mabivissey. As he stared, wondering at this, it was as if she stared back. She stared back and the portrait shifted. It *moved*.

Jojo dropped the leaf as a thousand leaves around him lit up, as each little face turned to look at him and with one voice they whispered: '*Who disturbs the peace of Mab?*'

Jojo began to run. But where? He took steps forward. Then left. Right.

'Trevor?'

But where to go? There were leaves everywhere. *She* was everywhere. He backed towards the nearest tree as the light of leaves died and grew, some flashed, some went dead. It was as if she had a million eyes trained to search for him.

He hit the tree with a thud. Trevor kept on yapping and throwing up leaves, lapping up water.

Jojo felt behind him. Something was not right here. This was no tree. No bark. Not wood. This was stone. Stone carved and shaped to be a natural, living thing. Not the real thing. Not real life. A copy. It looked good, but there was no life here.

Cold, dead river. Cold, dead trees. A cold, hard queen, sucking life from everywhere.

As Jojo thought this, a sound rumbled in the deep. A sound Jojo had heard before. The earth drummed and the ground shook. And behind him the stone began to shift. He did not need to turn to see what was coming from the rock.

The stone-men.

'Run, Trevor, run!' And with that, Jojo set off running himself. Trevor, ever the clever dog, joined him, then set off ahead of him, speeding uphill, for the stone forest sloped upward.

'Good boy,' Jojo called. 'That's it! Up.' If there was one thing he was sure of, it was that they must go up.

The boom of drums again. The ground reverberated below them. Jojo stumbled, almost fell. Above, the trees began to grow dim.

'Who disturbs the peace of Mab?' The whisper came from all around.

Still they ran, up through the streams, round the great dead trees. And little by little Jojo's lungs began to burn. He knew he couldn't go on much longer.

Another boom and this time a crack, as of thunder, as of the breaking of the world.

Jojo threw his hands up to his ears. His eyes squeezed shut.

Trevor barked and barked till Jojo opened his eyes again and on they ran. Onward. Onward. Up and up.

There were shadows now. Long, looming shadows. They ran ahead of the dog and the boy. Then the shadows died and fell back.

Another boom. Not from the ground now. From the rocks around them. From the trees.

Jojo's lungs were aflame. He could not go on.

'Who disturbs the peace of Mab?' came the whisper of leaves and Jojo could see the glinting of cold eyes glaring up at him as the shadows of the pursuing stone-men sprung up around him once more.

He must go on. He must. He ran again. A final spurt of energy. He knew it must take them on and out. Somewhere. There would be an opening. A gateway. They would reach safety. They must. They must. And then . . .

Boom! Crash! It was as if the whole world shook. Jojo's legs gave way. He came tumbling down onto the leaves and stony ground. His hands split open beneath him. His lungs burst. Shadow was all around him. The ground shook and shook as something came on great lumbering feet. And Jojo knew this was the end.

He mustered just enough energy to roll onto his back. Somewhere ahead of him, Trevor was stopping, skidding to a halt, coming bounding back to him.

No, boy! Jojo tried to say. But all that came was a wheeze of air. He knew now, in moments this would be a full-blown asthma attack. He knew this was the end.

The shadows deepened. The ground still rang with the beating feet of the stone-men. And it was not just shadows now. Jojo could see them.

They did not come fast. They did not need to. Three of them, all darkness and craggy rock, ready to crush him.

He reached into his pocket, for his pump. *May as well try for a final breath*, he thought.

But he had reached for the wrong pocket. Here was no asthma pump. Here was a pouch, a pouch which throbbed, warm glowing throbs like a miniature heart.

Gifts.

Was this hope rising in his chest? Welling in his eyes?

He pulled out the pouch. Loosened the string. It was the stone that pulsed. The holed stone. The hagstone. The stone for seeing the world as it was.

All was not as it seemed.

What else could he do? Apart from uselessly hurl the stone at the approaching stone-men.

He raised the hagstone to his right eye as the stone-men raised their fists, ready to strike.

And then he saw.

There were no trees. There was just Mab. She was there, thirty metres tall, towering over everything. She was there, a thousand of her – every eye turned towards him.

Then he saw.

There were no stone-men. There were just men. Three men who were one man. On the left, the man was dressed for a day at the beach in flip-flops and a T-shirt with tiny sailing boats printed all over it. The man on the right wore a builder's work trousers and a dusty black T-shirt. The man in the middle was dressed smartly. Jojo had seen him dressed like that before, on his wedding day.

Again, he could not stop himself: 'Dad!' he said. 'Dad. It's me. It's Jojo. It's your son.'

In his left eye he saw the stone-men stop.

In his right, his dad, all three images of his dad, shook themselves, blinked and then saw him too. Really saw him.

'Jojo?' they mouthed.

The trees around them shook. The lights came on all at once, blinding and brilliant. 'I see you!' they screamed, and with that the trees which were Queen Mab came crashing down.

Again, the boy squeezed his eyes shut. His body curled as if this could protect him. If he had any breath left, he would have screamed.

But nothing touched Jojo Locke. He opened his eyes. The stone-men – his dad – had thrown themselves over him and Trevor. The only light was from the leaves which burned below him.

She still watched.

Jojo put the hagstone up again. His father shouted at him: 'Go! Go!' His three faces were drenched in sweat. They were shaking with the effort of holding back the crushing stone ceiling.

Where could Jojo go? Where?

In answer, one of the stone-men Dads, the one who was dressed for his wedding, reached forward. His hands ripped at the stone earth. And the stone obeyed. It opened. Behind Jojo and Trevor, a tunnel opened.

'Dad,' Jojo said, his brow drawn tight. He couldn't leave without him. But was this like the flying boy? Just a mirage that would soon vanish?

'Go!' mouthed the stone Dads again.

Jojo and Trevor, with a squealing bark, leaped back as the shaking stone-men fell. As they collapsed as one. As the stone went back to being just stone.

And once again, all went dark.

The Boatman

All went dark apart from a cloud of shining golden dust. It came, Jojo had seen, from the heart of the central stone-man. From the heart of his dad.

The little golden cloud floated down towards him. He did not scramble back from where he lay on the smooth, cold floor. Just as he knew that the only way was up, he knew this little golden mist was here to help.

The specks rested on Jojo's chest then sunk into his wet T-shirt.

His lungs loosened. He breathed in: no pain, no burning. Then out. In and out. No asthma attack. No tightness at all.

'Thanks, Dad,' he whispered into the dark as a tear sprung to his eye. That couldn't be it. That wasn't his dad gone. It couldn't be. It just couldn't. On they would go.

'Trevor? Are you OK? Trevor?'

The dog didn't bark. He snuffled in close to Jojo, pushing his nose and then head under Jojo's arm, lifting him from a half-lying to a half-sitting position.

'You're right,' said Jojo. 'Let's go.'

Jojo reached around with his hands, fumbling, feeling what kind of place they now found themselves in. The floor seemed to be made of large rectangular flagstones. Behind was the collapsed stone which had been his dad, which had kept him safe from the trees of Queen Mab. Further on though, into the tunnel (had it already been there? Had his father, the stone-man, formed it?) the flagstones gave way to a huge step. It was as tall as three regular steps. Jojo found all this through touch. But as he lifted Trevor onto the step and then the step beyond, which curved to the left, and the step beyond that, which curved a little more, he found light slowly breaking in.

A warm red light again. Were they heading back into the forest?

Trevor farted each time Jojo lifted him, a little waft of stinky gas.

'Ah, Trevor,' Jojo said. 'You really do smell.' But he knew he wouldn't have it any other way. He knew he would not have made it this far without the dear dog. So he continued to carry him from step to step, up and up as they gently spiralled.

'Spiral stairs, Trevor, this feels more like a castle. We must be getting there.'

But as they rose and the light grew stronger and stronger, another feeling came over the pair. At first Jojo had put his sweat down to the exertions of lifting the dog before scrambling up himself. Lift and scramble, up the giant stairs, always curving left. But soon the warmth was not just prickling beneath their skin, it was in the air and in the stone too. The steps seemed hot somehow, like sand beneath your feet on a sunny day.

Trevor barked as Jojo put the dog down again on what must have been the fiftieth, sixtieth, maybe seventieth step.

'Yup, this is new,' said Jojo. He gulped and took a deep breath, the hot air drying his mouth.

How long since they had drunk something? He guessed they'd swallowed plenty of water as they struggled from the river in the cave. But he was thirsty now.

He wondered if he was unwise to run straight to the faerie mounds with nothing in hand. Was that really what Aunt Pen would have planned? Maybe a mission like this needed a full pack. Food. Supplies. How long would they be here? Would they find more and more Dads for hours, days, weeks? For ever?

How long would they be on these stairs?

Most of those questions Jojo had no answer to. But the last one soon became clear.

'I think that's the top,' Jojo said.

The stairs were well lit now. The heat was intense. Jojo's clothes had begun to dry from the river, but the dampness was soon replaced by his running sweat. Above they could see an opening. There was another chamber, not nearly as big as the forest, but all lit, as the stone woods had been, in an orange light. This light was not a glow though. This was a roaring blaze.

'Come on,' said Jojo, lifting Trevor one more time before his fear could get the better of him.

They climbed and climbed. The last steps leading them out.

Jojo found the source of the heat at once.

The chamber was almost like a station. The ceiling was at

least twenty metres up and carved into sweeping arches. The stairs they had climbed ran up onto a wide platform of sorts. Instead of rails though, the platform edge fell to a gently blipping pool of something that looked distinctly like . . .

'Lava!' Jojo said, placing a hand to steady Trevor, who barked and shuffled back towards the stairs.

The surface of the pool rippled and bubbled. It was black and orange and red and yellow. It swelled and moved, forming itself into shapes and patterns like clouds. There was a hand. Waves of red. An eye.

Jojo swallowed.

What now?

The platform area was closed at both ends. There were no more stairs. No doorway. The only way on appeared to be an arched entrance through which the lava flowed.

How could this be lava though? Surely they'd be burned alive this close.

Jojo took a step forward. It was still hot, still sweltering, but no hotter. He did not suddenly burst into flames.

It could not be real lava. Any more than they were real trees in that stone forest. Something like it, to be sure. But not the real thing. He imagined it could still burn though. If they touched it.

He took another step forward. Trevor farted and barked but didn't follow.

'Perhaps,' Jojo thought aloud, peering into the opening, 'there's . . . some way to go on.'

'I can take you on,' said a voice, deep and slow.

Jojo nearly jumped out of his skin. Trevor yapped and leaped up. He barked and ran in a quick circle.

There, in the lava pool, was a boat – six metres long and narrow with a carved prow. And at the back of the boat sat a man in a dark cloak.

How had Jojo not seen him before?

'You . . . you weren't there. Were you?' Jojo said.

The boatman dipped his head in a nod. 'I am always here.'

'But,' said Jojo, 'you weren't . . .' Then he thought again. 'Who are you?'

The boatman's head moved again, tipping to one side. 'Who am I?' he repeated, as if this question was the strangest he had heard. 'I am the boatman. I am always here.'

Jojo gulped. His heart was still hammering from the surprise of this boatman's appearance. But he'd seen so few people in this place – only her, Queen Mab, and him, his dad – it was quite a relief to meet someone else, even if it was a faceless stranger.

'Do you have a name though? I'm . . . I'm . . . Jojo.'

Again the boatman's cloak moved, his head tipping back to the other side. 'Jojo.' He nodded. 'That is a good name. A good name.'

Trevor had stopped barking. He was nudging Jojo's legs with his big, damp nose and letting out a rapid series of tiny farts.

The boatman seemed to lift his eyes to meet Jojo's now.

Jojo felt his gaze looking deep inside him. He swallowed hard and the boatman looked away.

'Do you want to go on?' said the stranger.

Jojo looked at the tunnel. The only way.

'On?' he said. 'Ye-yes. We do. We want to go on. Don't we, Trevor?'

He looked back at the dog. His tail was tucked firmly between his legs. His face was buried in the back of Jojo's knee.

'We do,' Jojo answered for the both of them and started towards the boat. 'Come on, boy.'

Trevor let out a small woof. He seemed to breathe in deep. He snuffled. Then he followed Jojo to the boat.

The boatman did not speak or move as the boy and the dog clambered in the boat. Although it had seemed narrow, it did not rock or bob. It did not seem to notice them climbing in at all. It certainly didn't sink further into the lava. It had not got any hotter either.

Then, without a word, the boatman stood and pushed away from the platform with a long pole that Jojo was sure had not been there before.

Trevor was at the front of the boat, Jojo in the middle and the boatman at the back. He dipped the long pole into the fake lava, pushing them forward. Then lifted it, strings of the red-hot substance swirling and falling back into the pool, and pushed again. In no time at all they were passing under the arch.

They were going on.

Lost and Found

The tunnel they passed along was not like the subterranean river, dark and cold. It was not like the forest, rough and wild. This tunnel, like the platform cavern, was carved and shaped. There were arches supported by tall pillars. Beams crisscrossed the ceiling. The walls were smooth.

Trevor spent his time looking ahead, past the prow figurehead, which was carved in some form, where the tunnel neither curved nor sloped. It just went on. Jojo was looking into the lava. He was sure those blips and bubbles were trying to form themselves into something more. Was there something in the lava?

Jojo dragged his eyes from the stream and looked to the boatman. There was no seeing into that deep hood.

'You can't have always been here,' said Jojo.

The boatman did not take his eyes from the way ahead. He kept on dipping and lifting the pole. There was a sound though, a deep breath being taken.

'I am always here. I have a debt to pay. I take people on.'

Jojo frowned. Sweat was dripping down his nose, running in little rivulets across his forehead. He looked from the boatman to Trevor to the front of the boat.

They had not inspected that figurehead. They'd been too

busy watching their step as they boarded the boat. But now he did—

'But perhaps once,' intoned the boatman. Jojo swept back round to look to the stranger. 'I was somewhere else.'

Maybe you were some*one* else, Jojo thought. He frowned again and reached for his pocket, reached for the hagstone. He felt and felt, but the stone was not there. He pulled out the pouch and looked inside. No stone. Just the coin. The last gift.

He had wondered for a moment if he were to look through the stone, what would he see? But he must have lost it, must have dropped it somewhere on the steps.

Again, Jojo found himself drawn to the surface of the lava. To the swirls and eddies in the burning river. There was the eye again. There was a mouth. Or did he imagine it? Was it like cloud-watching? You could see anything in the clouds if you looked long enough.

'Are we nearly there?' Jojo asked, still staring at the burning stream.

'Where?' asked the boatman.

Now Jojo looked up. 'You said, you'd take us on to . . . to . . .'

'I take people on. I have a debt to pay.'

Jojo looked back down the tunnel, the way they had come. There was no sign of the arch they had come through. The tunnel just went on. He looked ahead. Endless tunnel. He trained his eyes on the figurehead. It *was*. He could only see the back but he was sure now. It was her. Mab, carved on the prow of the boat.

The sweat now running down his back was not just from the heat. He shuffled a little towards the dog.

He turned again. His frown had deepened. 'Where do you take people?' he said to the boatman.

'I take them on.'

Jojo reached out a hand for Trevor. He needed to hold on to something. Here they were in the middle of a lava flow on a boat going . . . on.

'Where do we . . . do we stop?'

'I take you on.'

Jojo gulped. What was this? A boatman to take you nowhere? A debt?

He looked once more at the burning river. She was here. Eyes and hands and mouth and stream. Mab was here.

'Who are you?' he shouted at the boatman.

'I am the boatman.'

Jojo leaped up. He felt heat rising in him. Anger stronger than his fear. 'You're not a boatman.' In a few strides he was there, face to face with the stranger. He reached up and pulled down the hood.

The boatman did nothing to stop him. The boatman merely stared back with blank eyes, the eyes of Jojo's father.

'Dad,' gasped Jojo once more. Once more his father was here. He had found him again. Except this man was old. Not as old as Grandad. But old. Old and bald. Unlike the boy Dad, flying above the castle, and the young man Dad, who had been three stone-men, this Dad showed no sign that he recognised his son.

The boatman looked long at Jojo. Then he looked back to the tunnel ahead. He lifted the pole and dipped it once more. 'I am the boatman. I have a debt to pay. I take people on.'

'What now?' shouted Jojo. He twisted and shouted it at the figurehead. He shouted it at the river.

And a voice came back. 'He can never pay. The end will never come. HE IS MINE.'

The last three words came as jets of lava shooting from the surface of the lake, hitting the smooth stone walls and arched ceiling.

'Now you are too,' Queen Mab finished with a whisper.

Jojo was still standing. He licked his lips.

He was. He was hers, stuck on a boat going nowhere. No escape from this.

Except . . .

He knew what he had to do. Something that was hidden. A debt. Jojo smiled and the river of lava bubbled and hissed in reply.

Jojo reached into his pocket and once more pulled out the pouch. The river began to rock and froth, little waves hit the narrow boat. Trevor barked and stood, watching the lava warily. Jojo took the boatman's right hand from the pole. 'Look at me,' he said.

The boatman once more turned his gaze to the boy. His son.

'I found it,' Jojo said, emptying the little pouch into his father's hand. 'The coin. The payment.' Fresh spurts of lava erupted around them.

The many-sided, red-gold coin tumbled onto the boatman's palm. His eyes fixed upon it. He stared intently at the image of Queen Mab, which blazed in the light of the lava.

'Jojo,' the man said now in the voice of his father. 'You found it.' He looked at Jojo, a tear in his eyes, then back to the coin. He stared. He took a deep breath. 'And now my debt is paid.' The boatman, Jojo's dad, pushed the coin to the edge of his finger, caught it on the tip of his thumb and . . .

Flick! The coin sailed through the air. It turned end over end. Jojo saw it as if in slow motion – the head of Queen Mab, the engraved symbols, the queen, the symbols, the queen. It flew and then with a plop and a hiss it hit the lava stream.

Instantly, jets of lava erupted around them. The waves doubled in size, tripled. The boat rocked and twisted and began to smoke. The walls began to melt and then crumble.

'Now we've got to get out of here,' Jojo's dad shouted.

He plunged the pole back into the roiling river. He twisted and flicked the long boat sideways. They were now facing, not the long straight tunnel, but the wall.

'What are you doing?' shouted Jojo.

Trevor barked and barked over the coughing, roaring lava.

'Sometimes,' the boatman Dad called, pulling up the pole once more, 'the only way on is to smash straight through.' He pushed the pole downward with a mighty thrust and the boat shot forward. It rose on a wave. Another sent it rocking sideways.

Jojo reached out a hand and grabbed onto the dark cloak his father wore. He readied himself for the boat to smash into the falling stone of the wall. Behind them, the lava erupted again, not just a jet this time, though. Now it took form. Now it was a woman.

The boat jumped forward as a huge, fiery Queen Mab lunged for it.

'HE IS MINE,' the queen screamed, reaching for the boat. She did not grasp it though.

Jamie Locke, the boatman, pulled up the pole once more and with a leap, threw himself at the rearing faerie queen. The pole was a spear. It shot straight at her heart.

'No!' screamed Jojo. 'Noooo!' But there was nothing he could do.

The boat plummeted on. It hit the wall, not with a thud, not with a crash. There was no noise. No splintering of the boat. No falling wall smashing into them. In fact, there was no noise at all.

Jojo, who found he had squeezed his eyes tight shut, now opened them.

He found himself, bloody, bruised and burned, but still standing. In front of him was a huge stone door. Candles on metal stands stood on either side of the door. Trevor, his tail swishing against the tiled floor, bristled beside him. Behind him there was nothing but solid wall. That was no matter. Ahead was where he needed to go. Of that he was certain.

'We're here,' said Jojo. He tightened his fists and once more stepped forward. With a gulp he pushed the door open.

Fire

The door gave way and Jojo found himself gazing into a room he'd been in before. A circular room filled with pillars, each of which held a statue – a statue of his dad. As a boy running, a smile on his face. As a man, building something. A teenager swimming. There he was again on his wedding day.

Jojo stepped into the room, Trevor at his side. It was lit by a thousand flickering candles all on their own stands.

The last time he'd seen this room, with Aunt Pen on the first day he'd met her, he'd not been able to take in all the shimmering images in the stained-glass windows. (Just a week ago? It felt like an age.) Now they stood illuminated in his mind. Each image spoke to him.. There were sand dunes. A village green. There was London. Here was the arch at Dor beach. In each, there was another image of his dad, another memory. Here, he ran. There, he laughed. He read. He swam. He sat. He slept. He lived in the coloured glass.

Trevor barked and started forward.

'What is it, boy?' Jojo said. He looked over to where the dog had begun to trot.

They were not alone in that room. Sitting on one of a pair of silver thrones was an old, old man. His beard was white.

His brown skin was as crisp as dry leaves. He appeared to be asleep. But there was no mistaking him.

'Dad!' Jojo shouted. 'Dad!'

This had to be it. This *had* to be it.

The boy ran towards the throne and the sleeping man and the biggest stained-glass window of all. This was the only one that did not hold a memory of Jamie Locke. Instead, this window showed the faerie queen in her majesty. She was huge. Her flame-coloured hair filled the top of the window in waves like a mighty crown. She was dressed in red glass which bathed the place where the old man slept in a fiery glow. She stared as Jojo approached. But still he ran.

'Dad! DAD!'

He crossed the hall in moments. In a flash. He had found him.

'DAD!' he screamed once more.

The old man woke with a start. His eyes wide. He looked at Jojo, who now a step away, reached for him. And, without a word, he vanished.

But this time the room did not start to collapse. This time, the boy did.

'Noooo!' Jojo broke. His legs gave in. He fell, there on the cold tiles. He fell and sobbed and sobbed some more. Energy, what little was left of it, soaked through his ragged clothes and spilled out and away.

Trevor nudged him. Jojo pushed him away.

He could do no more.

'Take me home,' he whispered. 'Take me home.' Who did he say this to? To Aunt Pen? To Trevor? To his lost father? He didn't know. He didn't care.

Courage.

Where had it got him? He had flown, swum, climbed, raced through tunnel, forest and flame, and for what? For what?

The will to act.

Again and again he had pressed on. He had not stopped. On and on. And now . . . nothing. There was no more *on*. No doors, but the one he'd come through.

Fire in his belly.

Fire. Did he have it? Did he want it? He lifted his head from the floor.

Trevor let out a soft whine.

Jojo ignored the dog. Instead he looked up at the great queen in all her splendour.

'Fire!' he shouted. 'I'll show *you* fire!'

Jojo scrabbled upwards. He grabbed the arms of the silver chair and wrenched it from the floor. He lifted it high: the energy which had drained away now burst through his veins. He took a step, another, and with a great and final scream, hurled the throne at the stained-glass window. It shattered into an incalculable number of pieces and fell like beautifully coloured rain. Trevor leaped back but Jojo was not so fast. He put his arms across his face, but his already battered skin was torn and split in a dozen places.

It was some moments till the air cleared, till Jojo caught his breath. He could not believe what he'd done. And now he could not help himself. He let out a short laugh.

There, beyond the opening where the stained-glass window had been, was a walkway – a bridge out into the open sky and at the far end, beneath a stone gargoyle, a door.

'Sometimes,' Jojo said to himself, 'the only way on is to smash straight through.'

He wiped his eyes and only paused to pick up Trevor – there was glass everywhere. Then he ran forward, stepping out onto the bridge.

It was not a long bridge but it was narrow. There was no edge, no wall, no rail. It was just a stretch of stone. It ran, Jojo could see, from one of the castle towers – the biggest – to another. For the first time since they'd fallen through the clouds, Jojo was outside.

How long had passed? Hours? Days? He had no way to know. The sky was still that same purple and black swirling mass. Below was still an inky chasm.

Jojo looked up at the tower he made for. And then he saw: that was no gargoyle. The thing moved. It growled. It leaped from its guard post out onto the bridge.

It was a dog. It was a huge hellhound. It was all that Trevor was not.

Jojo had nothing. No weapon or shield or defence of any kind. Except one.

Before Jojo knew what was happening, the the little brown

terrier, the kindest dog Jojo had ever known, with an unfortunate case of irritable bowels, leaped from his arms with a deep growl and dashed forward like a hairy bullet.

'Trevor!' Jojo shouted. But there was nothing he could do. He could not match the dog for speed. And Trevor had thrown all his energy into that sprint.

He bounded forward, not as an overfed domestic dog, but as his ancestors, as a wolf. He snarled as he ran to the right, jumped to the left, opened his jaws and caught the vast beast's throat between his teeth.

Trevor clung on as the creature swung sideways, as his paw slipped on the edge of the bridge, as he rolled forward and downward. Trevor clung on as the two plummeted into the blackness below.

Like that, Trevor the good dog was gone.

Splinters Made Whole

For the second time in the space of a few minutes, Jojo fell to his knees. 'Trevor,' he wept. 'Not Trevor.'

Time passed. The clouds swirled. Jojo remained curled on the stone bridge.

What could he do? What could be done? Maybe . . . if he got back home . . . if he got to Aunt Pen . . . No. But he knew, he could not wish an end to . . . to death.

Trevor was gone.

It was a long time till Jojo stood and when he did, his legs buckled, he swayed. There was nothing to place a hand on so he took another deep breath. He drew himself up to full height and steadied himself.

Trevor would not die for nothing.

He wiped the back of his right hand across his eyes. It cleared the tears but left streaks of blood and soot across his face.

'Come on then,' he said to himself. He fixed the door in his sights and advanced. This had to be it. The final door.

Nine steps and he was there. The door was wooden, stained white. It had no handle, just a heavy metal knocker.

Jojo did not hesitate. He pulled back the knocker.

Bang. Bang. Bang.

There was a pause like the world taking a breath. And

then the door swung inward and Jojo stepped into the smallest room he had found himself in that day.

This really was a story-book room. This was the highest room of the tallest tower. Like the huge one before, it was round. It had a small window which let in the eerie purple light onto a raised four-poster bed. And on the bed lay, not a princess, but a man.

Jojo's dad.

Jojo took one step forward, opened his mouth and then stopped. He'd run to his dad too many times that day, called to him and then . . .

'What are you waiting for?' said a voice. It was soft and crackled, like the sound of autumn leaves beneath a bare foot.

Jojo turned to the woman who was sitting in a small wooden chair.

She was not a young girl. She was not a great queen. Like Aunt Pen, she was old and wizened and tiny. Streaks of red still showed through her white hair. Her skin was as white as paper.

'You!' Jojo said, his voice catching on the spiky balls of grief and anger welling in his throat. 'You did this. You did all of this!'

He stared at the old woman, who stared right back.

'I did,' she said eventually, her gaze falling to the man in the bed. 'I did. And . . . I'm sorry, Jojo Locke.'

Jojo had expected to face the queen at the last. But he had

expected Mab to be huge, to be glorious, to be terrible. But this . . . she was broken, like everything else.

'But why?' Jojo whispered, tears in his eyes. 'Why did you do it?'

Mabivissey kept her eyes on Jamie Locke, for this was the true Jamie Locke, his very centre. 'Love,' said the old faerie. 'I thought . . . *madness*. My own stubborn-headed stupidity.'

Jojo's frown deepened. He could not feel sorry for the old queen. But that bubbling cauldron of anger was beginning to cool. 'No!' he shouted, stoking the fire. 'You stole him. You stole my dad. Don't tell me you were just *stupid*.'

Mab's eyes slid from Jamie Locke's face to the floor, to the window. She took a deep breath.

'She said – my sister – you must not fall in love with a human. That has always led to destruction. She said it, but I did not listen. I thought I was too strong to be caught. But I was wrong. Madness had me before I knew it. I forgot who I was . . . what I was . . .'

Jojo looked at his father in the bed as the old faerie spoke. This was him. Jojo knew it. He was here. He'd found his dad and he would not leave this room without him.

'And I took the coin,' the tiny faerie went on. 'I would not let him die. Instead of showing him the way on, as I have done so many times, so many, many times, I would snatch Jamie from the jaws of death. I knew the time and so I waited and watched. I watched as Jamie forgot me. I watched as he met your mother. They fell in love. You came into the world.

I watched and my madness and my jealousy grew and grew. It took form and had magic of its own. My love became a mad dog within me and then without me.'

'By the time my sisters knew what I planned, it was too late. His time was up. I came and I took him. I brought him here and I used all my magic to seal him here. I thought that I had won.'

The faerie stopped. Jojo, still standing in the doorway, looked to Queen Mab. She stared at her shaking wrinkled hands.

'But you . . .' some pity for the faerie queen broke through Jojo's anger, 'you . . .'

'I lost,' she said. 'I broke everything. The laws of Elfhaeme and of your world. My duty. The bonds that tie the nine. My sisters. The very fabric of existence. And . . . myself. I broke myself, like glass shards of me and him, scattered.'

Jojo took a step towards the old woman on the chair. His head fell on one side as he inspected her again. She was not some great queen now. She was cracked and dying like everything else. The Queen Mabs he'd met, the shards of the faerie, terrible and beautiful, were not here, just this ancient husk of a woman. She was *empty*.

'As you see it, Jojo Locke, I became raging splinters of jealousy and rage. And your father, he became memory – stolen from your world, from his parents, from your mother, from you, and frozen here in stone and glass.'

Jojo saw then the statues and the stained-glass windows

for what they were – not just the echo of what had once been, but the very substance of it, all the light and dark, the love and warmth, the memory itself.

The old faerie looked at Jojo for the first time since he had come in. She nodded. 'And we were locked here. By the monsters I'd created.'

Jojo could see that she truly was Aunt Pen's sister. They may have had different-coloured skin and hair, but in every other way they were almost twins.

'Your own magic kept you both here?'

She nodded again. 'And I waited,' she said. 'I tried to get one message to my sister. The wisest of us all, who sees all that has come before, Penperro. But . . .' The old faerie trailed off and Jojo wondered if she was done, if she too had gone, like Aunt Pen before her. Finally she sighed. 'In the end all she could do was flee. It was that, or be destroyed, like so many of the Elfhaeme.' Tears were rolling down the wrinkled cheeks of the faerie queen. 'And I wondered . . . wondered if she could . . .' Mab stopped again.

'She sent me,' said Jojo.

'There is her wisdom,' said Mab. 'There's so much I've broken. But some things are stronger even than magic. Blood was needed. And now . . . now . . . you're here.'

Jojo looked down at his hands, lined with little cuts and grazes. He'd sure brought blood.

'Blood calling to blood. The blood of the man given in love, to bring him back. Only a son or daughter could do this thing. Penperro, it seems, waited till the last, till you were old enough and her magic was not yet gone.'

'It's gone now,' said Jojo. 'I think . . . I think . . . she's gone. She died . . . I think.'

The faerie queen frowned and looked down again at her own hands. 'One act of stupidity, of stubbornness, of madness,' she whispered. 'Dear Penperro.' Then, without looking back up, she said, 'Please take him.'

Jojo looked at his father. 'How?'

'Simply touch him,' Mab said. 'Call him. Blood will call to blood.'

Jojo looked once more at the faerie who still stared at her own hands. Tears still fell from her crinkled eyes. Then he turned back to his father.

'And if I do,' Jojo said, 'I will put right what went wrong.' Jojo knew now what that meant. Hopes had risen in the days gone past of a father returned. But Jojo knew now.

'You will,' said the queen of death. 'My act will be undone.'

'And . . . my father . . .' Jojo knew the truth. He was not here to rescue his father. He could not bring him back. He was here to put right what went wrong. 'My dad will die on Trestle Beach.' The words hung in the air. Now spoken, they could not go back. There was only one glint of hope in that darkness. 'But we will remember. We will all remember.'

Jojo's eyes had filled with tears, they ran down his cheeks and burned his cut skin.

'It is the only way,' whispered Mab. 'He will die but he will no longer be gone. He will be where he belongs, in your mind and your heart, with the ones he loved, those he left behind.'

Jojo hesitated. He wanted his dad. There was only one way to have him back. Memory, alive and breathing, in his mind.

Just a few steps and he was there, by the bedside. He took his father's hand. It was warm – the last embers of a guttering fire. Jojo gulped and whispered, 'Dad?'

Then, as if by magic, Jamie Locke woke up.

He woke and stared at his son. And as he stared, the years rolled back. His wrinkles smoothed. His grey hair fell and left in its place tight black curls. Jamie Locke breathed in deep. He breathed in. He sighed. Then opened his mouth and whispered, a look of questioning across his face, 'Jojo? Is that you?'

Jojo held his dad's hand in both of his own. 'Dad,' he said once more. 'It's me. It's Jojo.'

Father and son stared at each other. Until Jojo felt a tug, felt a pull backwards. He clung onto his dad. He clung on. 'Dad?'

Jamie Locke then spoke for the final time. 'Don't worry, little man. Don't look back. It's going to be OK. Live, Jojo. Live. Remember, always. But look forward and live.'

Then, for one final time, Jamie Locke disappeared from the Land of Faerie.

Some invisible force still pulled at Jojo as hot streaming tears poured from his eyes. He looked to the chair where the faerie queen Mab had sat, but she too had gone.

Again, Jojo was tugged backwards and now he could not resist. He slid to the door and out onto the bridge. He was lifted from his feet and now he flew through the broken window, past the remaining silver throne and through the great hall.

It was not just Jojo being dragged out of place. Each statue was up and spinning through the air. The glass panes began to dislodge themselves and join the waltz of objects flying around the room.

Jojo was whipped onwards, through the great door, into the dark. He sped up now, soaring over the river of lava. He spun down the spiral stairs, smashed through the rock which had once been the stone-men and then shot past trees and streams. The leaves were not falling now, they were rising up, sucked from the floor.

Time was in reverse.

Jojo hurtled down the tunnel, ducked once into the river, then he was out, flying backwards across the abyss. Except it was not an abyss any longer.

Hills and fields, rivers and towns were rising up out of the chasm. They churned like the surface of a stormy sea as Jojo flew overhead.

From the towers of the castle, great spurts were erupting. It was a multicoloured volcano. As these sprays spread, Jojo realised they were not lava or liquid. They were creatures – faeries and goblins and piskies, others too that Jojo had no name for, some big, some tiny, flesh and blood and rock and wood – the inhabitants of Elfhaeme. There were animals too – every kind of animal, great and small. They squeaked and squawked, barked and bayed and talked in voices like his own as they flew in every direction.

There was a place for everything and everything would go back to its rightful place. Jojo realised he had only now begun to scratch the surface of that place. It was a whole world that would take an eternity to fully know.

He picked up speed as the clouds, the purple and black clouds, went in the opposite direction, feeding themselves back into the distant castle.

The sun broke out over that strange land. And Jojo just caught a glimpse of the village which had been abandoned when last he saw it, now alive with people – if that was the right word for them – of all shapes and sizes, as he flew into the dark.

Back

Jojo opened his eyes to an empty room. It was unrecognisable at first. There were no Tottenham Hotspur posters on the walls. No clothes on the floor. No chest of drawers covered in every kind of thing an eleven-year-old boy covers his chest of drawers with.

'Come on, Jojo,' a voice called.

He was lost. He was shaken. Like he had woken with a start from some now-fading dream. He did not at first answer to his mum's voice.

'Jojo?' she called again. 'You in there? Said your goodbyes? Come on!'

Said his goodbyes. Said his *goodbyes*?

And then he remembered. Jojo had just finished Year 6, he was off to secondary school in September and just like Dad had always planned, they were saying goodbye to London.

It had taken weeks but they were all packed up. Everything the Lockes owned was packed in a van parked on the street outside. Mum had packed in her job. They had packed the final days with goodbyes to all they'd miss in London.

Even though Dad had been gone for six years, they kept him alive, they always remembered and they always looked forward to this day.

For all the Lockes, even Lizzie, who'd lived her life in London, the move to Dor was like going home. They were taking Dad home.

'Coming, Mum,' Jojo called. He stood, his head swam a moment, but he soon steadied himself. It was very strange. But Jojo was utterly exhausted. He'd sleep on the train, he thought to himself, as he stumbled out of his bedroom and into the empty lounge.

Ricco was there, a rucksack on his back. Mum was there, grinning from ear to ear. She'd said goodbye to sharp business suits and wore a summer dress of yellow and pink.

'Let's go,' Mum said. 'Grandad and Grandma are expecting us for lunch.'

'And Trevor,' Ricco said.

Trevor. A lump rose in Jojo's throat. A tear swelled in his eye. And a feeling of deep relief came over him. And he remembered. Everything.

Lizzie Locke looked at her eldest son, a frown breaking across her face – was he ready for this move?

'You OK, buddy?' Mum said.

Jojo took a deep breath. He remembered what no one else did. He remembered the faerie. He remembered the land beyond. He remembered the House of the Nine. And he remembered the great, vast chasm where Dad should have been. And now he was there. Jojo remembered everything. Jojo looked at his mum through shining eyes. He nodded. 'Yeah,' he said. 'I am. I'm really ready.'

Lizzie squeezed Jojo in a hug.

'He'd be really pleased, Mum,' Jojo said just for her ears. 'Dad . . .' His words ran out but Lizzie's had not.

She always talked about Dad. Told the boys all about him. Told them all the ways they were like him. Even Ricco, who'd never met him, knew him so well from every retold memory, every story, every well-pawed photo.

Dad might be gone but the place where he'd been was full-to-overflowing.

'He would be really pleased,' Mum said. 'And so, so very proud of you, Jojo. Remember that. Always remember that.'

And with those final words, the Lockes left London.

Summer Moon Sets

It was the first night of holidays, that night on the brink of long summer days, days when anything could happen, days when magic is in the air.

It was full, the moon that night. And the sky over the lane in Dor was filled with stars – not a cloud in sight. If Jojo had gone to his window in the top bedroom of the new house, which Mum had spent six years pouring every scrap of money she could muster into building, he would have had a clear view across the field to the tree that marked the place where Dad was buried and to a man dressed in black, who stared up at the top window, Jojo's window.

Once again the Sandman was waiting for someone. He knew they'd come. Just as he had.

As he waited, he reached into the little sack on his belt and pulled out a few specks of golden dust. He put them to his lips and blew. The specks swam and glittered, spun and twisted their way on the breeze towards the house and the cottage. They found their way through letterboxes, upstairs to the sleeping Lockes. And here they came to rest, giving dreams of fishing trips and wild woods, of the wedding in this very field, of a sleeping, dusty man on a sofa, of birthdays and summer days and just plain old ordinary days. Jojo dreamed of Dad.

'Here we are again then, Sandman,' said a voice from beside the man in black.

The Sandman did not answer. Nor did he look down. 'Here we are,' he said.

'We did it,' said the small woman dressed as a tiny pirate.

'We did,' said the Sandman.

'Ever the conversationalist, aren't you,' Penperro said under her breath. 'You'll want to know of home, I imagine?' The Sandman did not answer but the queen of memory knew what filled his own dreams. 'It's all back,' she said. 'The fields green, the trees tall, the mountains misty. Many have come back home. Piskies once more fly, hobs are busy in every home and faeries sing.'

The Sandman offered a single nod.

'There's eight thrones returned to the House of the Nine. Five of the sisters sit on them. Aoede and Melete still sleep. Mabivissey has joined them till she is ready to be born again to redeem herself. Only Acciona Polperra remains at sea.'

At this, the Sandman took a deep breath.

'You could come home?'

If one could look beneath that hood, you'd have seen a worn and weary face drawn in a deep frown. 'As long as she is lost, I will keep my watch,' he whispered.

'Well,' said Penperro, 'I've been thinking about that. Now there is once again a faerie knight . . . perhaps *he* could help.'

Two pairs of faerie eyes turned to the top window of the

247

house the Lockes called home. To the bedroom of the faerie knight.

'Perhaps,' said the Sandman. 'Perhaps.' And then he was gone.

'Goodbye, brother,' whispered the curiously dressed faerie with the gold hoop earrings and the many packages, parcels, bags and bundles hanging from her shoulders. Then with a wrinkle of her nose, a blink of her eyes and a flash of light, she too was gone.

Acknowledgements

I am immensely grateful to the whole team at Andersen Press for the care and dedication put into making this book a reality. There are many of you working on cover and text and sales and rights and everything in between. And to each of you I am thankful. There are two of the team to whom I'd like to give a special thanks. Charlie Sheppard, a few words of encouragement you extended at just the right time meant more than you know; your trust and belief kept me writing. Finally, Eloise Wilson, this book would certainly not be here without you. Your insights have been invaluable but more so your kindness and patience. Thank you.

SEASON OF SECRETS

SALLY NICHOLLS

On a wild and stormy night Molly runs away from her grandparents' house. Her dad has sent her to live there until he Sorts Things Out at home now her mother has passed away. In the howling darkness, Molly sees a desperate figure running for his life from a terrifying midnight hunt. But who is he? Why has he come? And can he heal her heartbreak?

'A stand-out story . . . exciting [and] profound'
Guardian

'A wonderful, evocative, lively book'
Literary Review

9781839130465